The
Time-Traveling
Fashionista

AND CLEOPATRA, QUEEN OF THE NILE

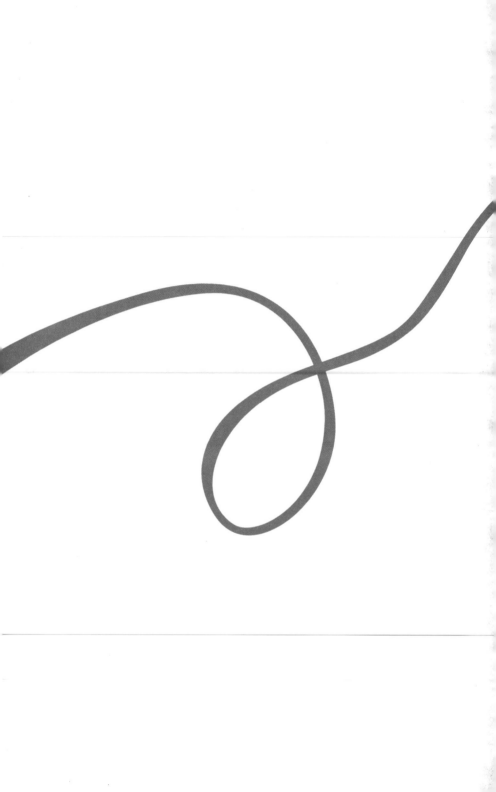

The Time-Traveling Fashionista

AND CLEOPATRA, QUEEN OF THE NILE

a novel by

BIANCA TURETSKY

poppy

LITTLE, BROWN AND COMPANY

New York Boston

Also by Bianca Turetsky:

The Time-Traveling Fashionista On Board the Titanic

The Time-Traveling Fashionista at the Palace of Marie Antoinette

Text copyright © 2013 by Bianca Turetsky
Illustrations copyright © 2013 by Sandra Suy
THE TIME-TRAVELING FASHIONISTA® is a registered trademark of Bianca Turetsky. All rights reserved.

Poppy

Hachette Book Group
237 Park Avenue, New York, NY 10017
Visit our website at www.lb-kids.com

Poppy is an imprint of Little, Brown and Company.
The Poppy name and logo are trademarks of Hachette Book Group, Inc.

The publisher is not responsible for websites (or their content) that are not owned by the publisher.

First Edition: December 2013

Library of Congress Cataloging-in-Publication Data

Turetsky, Bianca.
    The time-traveling fashionista and Cleopatra, queen of the Nile : a novel / by Bianca Turetsky ; illustrations by Sandra Suy.—First edition.
        pages cm
    Summary: After trying on a Grecian dress, a twelve-year-old girl who likes vintage fashion travels back to ancient Egypt, where she experiences life as a handmaiden to Queen Cleopatra and learns valuable lessons about confidence and leadership.
    ISBN 978-0-316-22488-8
    [1. Time travel—Fiction. 2. Fashion—Fiction. 3. Cleopatra, Queen of Egypt, d. 30 B.C.—Fiction. 4. Egypt—History—332–30 B.C.—Fiction.] I. Suy, Sandra, illustrator. II. Title.
    PZ7.T8385Tip 2013
    [Fic]—dc23
                                                                                2012042009

10 9 8 7 6 5 4 3 2 1

SC

Book design by Alison Impey

Printed in China

For my parents,
with love

"You can have anything you want
in life if you dress for it."

EDITH HEAD,
Academy Award–winning
costume designer

CHAPTER 1

"Louise, what are you doing awake at this hour? What was that noise?" Her mother's concerned voice was calling to her from directly outside her bedroom door.

"Nothing, Mom!" Louise replied, startled, dropping the black poodle necklace back into the steamer trunk with a clatter. "I couldn't sleep, so I started reorganizing my clothes. I'll go back to bed now." She ran out of her closet, dove into her canopy bed, buried herself under her grandmother's quilt, and held her breath. She was often switching up her vintage collection by decade, designer, and color, and she hoped for the time being her mother would buy that excuse. She heard the doorknob turn halfway and then stop, as though Mrs. Lambert had changed her mind midthought.

"Very well. Try to sleep, Louise. You've had a long day, and it is a school night, you know."

Louise let out her breath. "I know," she croaked. But

it wasn't just an ordinary school night. In the course of the last fifteen minutes, the axis of Louise's world had completely tilted. For some reason, her mom owned a necklace identical to the ones worn by Marla and Glenda, her magical Traveling Fashionista stylists. It was such a unique piece; it couldn't just be a coincidence! Her own mother—the one who constantly gave her a hard time about her vintage collection, who was always trying to drag her along to some boring department store, who almost forbade her from attending the Traveling Fashionista Vintage Sale in the first place—was somehow in an old, wrinkled, and yellowing photograph wearing a long, antique white dress layered with scalloped lace trim, with a horse-drawn carriage rolling past in the background. She thought her mother was old, but not *that* old. Unless the photograph was taken at a state fair or on a movie set, her proper, English, pearl-and-sweater-set-wearing mother was quite possibly a Traveling Fashionista herself!

"Isn't it in your family, too?"

Stella, a thirteen-year-old Traveling Fashionista, had asked Louise that question in the grand halls of the palace of Versailles. It reverberated in her mind like an echo. But Stella's great-great-aunt twice removed was Coco Chanel! Louise's mother was just…her mom. Or at least that was what she had thought, up until that night. It seemed as though her mother had a much more interesting history than Louise could have

imagined. She clutched the worn patchwork quilt to her chest with nervous anticipation, trying to reconcile the familiar image of the posh and formal mom she thought she knew with the smiling, vintage-clad Victoria Lambert in the black-and-white photograph. It was impossible.

Her mind raced back to her own time-traveling experiences—the excitement at receiving the mysterious purple invitation to the first sale, trying on Miss Baxter's enchanted pink gown, waking up on the A deck of the *Titanic*, hitting the iceberg.... And then her second trip, taking her back to Versailles in a hooped blue dress, living in luxury as part of the royal court of Louis XVI. The tingly, electric feeling of trying on those dresses, their silky fabric charged with memories of the women who wore them before she did. Faces of the people she met on her adventures flashed through her head like credits in a movie: Marla and Glenda; Miss Baxter; Benjamin Guggenheim; the oblivious Marie Antoinette; Louise's gardener crush, Pierre; Stella with her braces and corseted dress; and then, finally, her mother. Louise wasn't quite sure yet how she fit into this story line.

As her memory traced back over her adventures, Louise drifted off and eventually fell into a sleep so deep she didn't even dream.

CHAPTER 2

At 7:13 AM, minutes before her alarm, Louise was woken up by the intoxicating smell of frying bacon. Was this actually her house? Quaker Oats had never smelled so good. Despite getting only a few hours of sleep, Louise jumped out of bed and bounded down the creaking main staircase toward the unfamiliarly delicious aroma, half wondering if she was still asleep. *Wait, can you even smell in dreams?* she pondered as she walked into the spacious old kitchen.

Her father was standing at the stove wearing a white chef's apron over his gray-and-purple NYU T-shirt, holding a spatula and flipping pancakes. His wire-rimmed glasses were a little foggy from the steam rising from the griddle. He thrust a glass of freshly squeezed orange juice into her hands.

"Morning, chicken," Louise's father cheerfully greeted her, using his completely random and embarrassing nickname for his only daughter. "You're up bright and early."

"Dad, it's a school day. It's not like this is a conscious choice. What...what's going on?" Louise asked, confused to not see her mom stirring a cast-iron pot of bland, lumpy oatmeal as she did every morning. She took a gulp of the sweet, pulpy juice. *Yum.*

"Well, I figured if I'm not going into the office, I can focus on my other interests and maybe give cooking a try." Mr. Lambert had recently been let go from his law firm, Gladstone, Braden LLP, in a case of corporate downsizing and was currently unemployed, much to her mother's anxiety. On one hand it meant they didn't have enough money to send Louise on her class trip to France, but on the other it also meant she would get to see her dad a lot more because he wasn't working long hours at the office. And with his daily commute from Manhattan to Fairview, their quaint suburban town an hour outside the city, he rarely made it home for supper. Besides, Louise had gotten to experience Paris in her own way, even if the Paris of the seventeen hundreds was a far dirtier and less romantic city than what she had expected. It was probably very different today.

"Awesome!" Louise exclaimed, grabbing the plate of blueberry pancakes and crisp bacon that her dad had just placed on the granite countertop. "Where's Mom?" she asked as she settled into the sunny breakfast nook and dove into her unexpected morning feast. She had some serious questions to ask her mother.

"She went to the market. I'm taking over breakfast duty for the foreseeable future. Dinner as well. I assume you don't have any objections?" her silver-haired dad asked with a smile. Mrs. Lambert was a notoriously horrible cook, and Louise was happy to not have to be tortured with whatever inedible concoction she put on the table. Everything was inevitably doused in malt vinegar, her English mother's favorite condiment.

Louise gave her dad an enthusiastic thumbs-up while her mouth was crammed full of syrupy blueberry deliciousness, but she couldn't help feeling the timing was a little odd. Her mom was always home in the morning, forcing a balanced meal on her and warning her about missing the bus. It was their routine, and this was the one day when Louise really did need that mother-daughter time. She had some majorly important stuff to discuss with her. Like where did she get the black poodle necklace and antique photograph Louise had found last night in the old steamer trunk? Now all her questions would have to wait until tonight after she got home from swim practice.

"What time does the bus come, anyway?" her dad asked offhandedly as he placed another stack of pancakes on her plate. Alarmed, Louise glanced up at the kitchen clock.

"Ummm, about five minutes ago," she answered, having completely lost track of time without her mother, the morning drill sergeant, breathing down her neck.

Momentary concern flashed across her dad's blue-gray eyes. "Oh, well, I can't imagine you've ever been late before. Go hurry up and get ready. I'll give you a ride to school."

"Thanks, Dad," she said, rushing out of the kitchen to get dressed and snap a Polaroid. With everything going on, Louise had almost forgotten her daily routine. She had a feeling that in her haste she had cut off the top part of her head, but she didn't have time to wait for the milky gray film to come into focus. She shoved it into her sock drawer with the rest of the photos. Louise knew she was growing up on the inside, and one day soon she was sure she would see an actual physical difference on the outside, too. She wanted a record of when that moment finally happened.

Before heading back downstairs, Louise ripped a page off her daily Virgo horoscope calendar: "It's not always the most beautiful girl in the room who has the most power; rely on your wits to wow the crowd." *Is my horoscope, like, trying to tell me something?* she wondered, glancing at her all-too-familiar reflection in her full-length mirror. Louise had come to accept that she was never the most beautiful girl in the room, not that she thought about it a lot, but still, the reminder was a little depressing. She hardly ever attempted to wear her naturally frizzy hair down. Because of daily after-school swim practice, her flyaway curls were wet half the time anyway, so she pulled them back into a tight little bun at the nape of her neck. Her teeth were still masked by ugly metal braces, making her smile resemble more of a tight-lipped grimace. She was boy-skinny, with disproportionately broad swimmer shoulders, and basically felt that her body was doing its best to annoy her in every way.

The only thing she felt she had any control over was what she wore. And Louise took that very seriously. Shopping, researching, and scouring thrift stores for vintage finds was her obsession. Her walk-in closet was filling up with her ever-expanding vintage collection. Since no one else at her school seemed to share her passion, a lot of her quirkier pieces were reserved for dancing around in her bedroom alone. But she felt as if life would catch up with her one day, and she would have just the place to wear a flapper dress from the Roaring Twenties with its matching sequined headband.

Of course, school was not that place, and this morning, Louise opted for a pale green seventies-style dress with little white-and-yellow daisies embroidered on it, swapping in black leather ballet flats for her usual neon pink Converse All Stars. She grabbed her worn purple backpack, tossed a few red and yellow flakes for her goldfish, Marlon, into the round bowl, and sprinted back down the stairs. She was definitely going to be late for homeroom.

Louise and her dad pulled out of the driveway just as Mrs. Lambert's car turned the corner onto their road. Louise felt as if she didn't even know who her own mother was anymore. It was strange to leave without giving her a kiss good-bye.

CHAPTER 3

After a mind-numbingly dull school morning—highlighted by a supereasy math quiz and a forty-minute presentation on the life cycle of phytoplankton—Louise met up with her best friend, Brooke Patterson, at their neighboring lockers to switch out their books for end-of-day classes. Louise smiled as she unhooked her combination lock and opened the flimsy door. Glancing into Brooke's organized, uncluttered locker, with its neat stack of textbooks, a ballpoint pen, extra lip gloss, and a large magnetic mirror hanging inside the otherwise undecorated beige metal door, Louise thought how amazing it was that she and Brooke were friends even though they were so different. Louise's locker, by contrast, was like a peek into her cluttered and chaotic brain—images of iconic actors and models from different decades formed an overlapping Scotch-taped collage, and a balled-up Indian print scarf was partially hidden under a lopsided pile of loose-leaf notebooks full of dress designs that she had doodled in class in lieu of actual notes. Luckily, despite her lack of notes and fleeting attention span, she was still a straight-A student and always turned in her assignments on time. Nonetheless, she realized she could probably stand to be a bit more organized. She suddenly felt overwhelmed and slammed her locker shut, vowing to clean it out before the weekend.

"See you at swim practice?" Louise asked Brooke, although it wasn't really a question. Of course she would—that's what they did on Monday afternoons.

"Actually, Kip and I were going to hang out after school today," Brooke said, averting her pale blue eyes. Kip and Louise's best friend had gone to the seventh-grade semiformal dance together, and Brooke had spent a good part of her fancy-dress thirteenth birthday party talking and flirting with him. But it was not as if they were actually together or anything, or that's what Louise had thought up until about a second ago.

"You're skipping swim practice to hang out with...a boy? Is that what happens when you turn thirteen? You lose your mind?"

"It's just one swim practice," Brooke replied defensively.

"I feel like we're in an after-school special," Louise said sadly. "Called *Boy Crazy*. And it doesn't end well."

"Don't be so dramatic, Lou," Brooke said, trying to sound

casual as she expertly pulled her sun-streaked blonde hair up into a high ponytail. "Our lives are not a Lifetime movie."

"And what exactly should I tell Coach Murphy?" Louise asked, realizing once she'd said it that she was starting to sound a lot less like Brooke's friend and more like her mother.

"Nothing. He won't even notice."

"Okay, now you've officially lost it."

"Tell him I have an after-school study group or something. Be creative. You're good at that."

Louise was the creative one; Brooke was the popular one with the cute lacrosse-playing boyfriend named Kip. The roles were defined, and the feeling that she and her best friend were growing apart was crushing Louise's chest like a lead weight. "Fine, but just this once," Louise conceded.

The warning bell rang, and the clusters of students gathered in the corridor began to disband. The girls spotted Brooke's cousin Peter across the crowded hall with his schedule and a pile of books. He looked lost and was almost knocked over by the wave of kids rushing off to class.

"Go help him," Brooke nudged as she gave her perfect reflection one last signature Brooke Patterson pout and slammed her locker shut. She gave her befuddled cousin a wave over her shoulder and took off for her own class.

Louise had met Peter just the other day at Brooke's

thirteenth birthday party. He was an eighth-grade transfer student from Boston and pretty cute. He also bore a striking resemblance to Pierre, the French gardener Louise had befriended and had a major crush on at the palace of Versailles. She swore she'd been transported there *for real* after trying on a robin's egg blue antique dress at the last Fashionista Sale. It seemed crazy under the harsh fluorescent lights of Fairview Junior High, but Louise couldn't help but wonder if somehow Peter *was* Pierre. Another Traveling Fashionista in her own school! Peter looked up and smiled sheepishly as he saw Louise approach.

She was only a few steps away from him when she tripped, nearly flinging her armful of books at his face. *How is that even possible?!* she wondered. *I'm wearing ballet flats!* She willed her ears to cool down and not totally betray how embarrassed she felt inside.

"Hey, are you okay?" Peter asked, looking genuinely concerned.

"Yup, I think so," Louise said, before starting to laugh hysterically, something she tended to do at inappropriate times.

"In that case, do you know where Gym B is?" he asked. "Looks like I have fitness next."

"Sure, I'll show you. This place is a bit of a maze at first," Louise said with an encouraging smile, happy that he seemed a little insecure, too. "But you should put that map away. You don't want to look like a sixth grader." Sixth grade was only last year, but sometimes it felt like another lifetime.

"Thanks," Peter replied gratefully, shoving the map into his gray canvas messenger bag and pulling an old-fashioned bronze pocket watch from the green army jacket he was wearing. "I guess I'm a little late. Seems to be the theme of my day."

"Where did you get that watch?" Louise asked him curiously, recognizing it from when they first met. "It's amazing." It looked really old, but in a good, vintage way. Like something she would buy.

"Oh, this? It used to be my grandfather's. He lives in France. My parents would love to throw it out, though. They can't stand old stuff."

"I know what you mean," Louise replied. *Or I used to*, she corrected herself. "Is that where your family's from? I mean, before Boston."

"Originally France. At least my dad's family was. I'm Peter Moreau VII. Well, actually, my grandfather is Pierre, and then my family Americanized it to Peter. I'd love to know more about my family history, but all that's managed to stick around is a name and this old pocket watch."

Louise gasped. "Maybe your family was involved in the French Revolution or something," she blurted out. She had a feeling she had met Peter's great-great-great-great-grandfather working in the garden of Versailles during the French

Revolution. And he was totally hot. Apparently those dimples were genetic.

"I doubt it, but that would be awesome. Oh, and my mom and Brooke's mom are sisters, but I guess you knew that already," he continued, seemingly oblivious to Louise's flustered reaction.

As Peter tucked the pocket watch back into his jacket, the final bell rang, signaling that anyone hearing it and still in the hallway had better start preparing a good excuse for being late.

Hearing Peter's brief description of his family history, Louise realized that he probably wasn't a Traveling Fashionista, but he loved history and she felt strangely connected to him anyway through her last adventure. It was a different feeling from the butterflies she got around Todd Berkowitz. It seemed as if Peter could really *get* her. But just as she started to think about what that meant, Louise heard a skateboard wheeling down the hallway. On his skateboard, Todd was a little taller than Louise, which was still not that tall. He was wearing another of his oversize striped polo shirts, and it was amazing that his baggy pants didn't fall down to his New Balance sneakers.

"Hey, Louise!" he called, coming to a stop a little in front of her. "What about those french fries? Josh, Tiff, and I are going to the food court after school Wednesday. Wanna come?"

Josh? And more important, *Tiff*? Okay, so the "date" she had been imagining and mentally planning her outfit for since Brooke's birthday party was actually a group thing. With Tiff, no less, the blonde California transfer student Todd had been spending a lot of his time with. Louise was annoyingly jealous. Maybe she'd misread the whole thing and he just thought of her as one of the guys after all.

"Ummm...maybe?" Louise responded. She didn't have the time to think about it. She had so many other things boggling her mind right now. Like her mother. Like Peter and his French connection.

"Cool. Text me!" Todd said casually, pushing off on his skateboard and gliding down the hall.

"Come on, Peter. I have history next, but I'll show you to your class," Louise said, taking off toward the gym.

"I love history," Peter replied as they ran through the now empty corridor. Peter was new, so he had an excuse for being late, but Louise was going to have some explaining to do— unfortunately to Miss Morris, whose class had recently become a lot more interesting.

After her elderly teacher's lecture about the *Titanic*, Louise soon found herself on board that ill-fated ship; and after a lesson on the French Revolution, Louise had somehow become a member of Marie Antoinette's inner circle in eighteenth-century France. She couldn't wait to see what possible adventures were in store for her next, and she had a feeling that Miss Morris's upcoming lesson might have the answer!

CHAPTER 4

"As you can see, I am not Miss Morris."

"That's for sure!" shaggy-haired Billy Robertson, class clown and Louise's nemesis, yelled from his seat at the back of the room. The whole class snickered. Since the beginning of the school year, Billy had made it his personal mission to annoy and embarrass Louise on their twice-daily bus ride, mainly about whatever vintage outfit she happened to be wearing that day. She knew she shouldn't care what he thought, but it still made her insecure about her fashion choices. It wasn't the most inspiring way to start the morning, to say the least.

"My name is Miss Jones, and as I was called only this morning to take over the class for the rest of the term, I don't have a lesson planned for today," the substitute continued, pushing her big, round reading glasses up into her curly red hair.

"The rest of the year? Is she, like, dead?" Billy asked as the class laughed again, but nervously this time. Considering how old Miss Morris was, that question didn't seem so funny.

"It's a bit odd, but it seems that your teacher has decided to start her summer vacation early and take a little trip. She said something about wanting to walk among the pharaohs and heading off to see the Great Pyramids. Rather peculiar, but in any case I am your new history teacher. I graduated last year from Brown University, where I majored in world history with a focus on antiquities. I'm excited to get to know all of you with the little bit of time we have left before summer vacation." At the mere mention of the words *summer vacation*, a new, excited energy was injected into the otherwise lifeless room. "Now quiet, please. Why don't we go around the class and you can tell me your name and something special about yourself."

Louise felt her face already start to flush with anxiety. Miss Jones was young and optimistic, the kind of teacher who thought these getting-to-know-you games could actually help you get to know anyone. In Louise's opinion, they were just embarrassing.

Hi, I'm Louise Lambert and I'm a Traveling Fashionista. If people actually told the truth about themselves, it could be a really scary game. *My name is Louise and I'm on the swim team and I like vintage fashion*, she rehearsed in her head. That was

24

easier; that made sense. Even if at Fairview Junior High, vintage clothing was still considered a little weird, particularly to Billy, whose fashion sense didn't extend beyond the same baggy jeans and dirt brown or navy pullover sweater he wore practically every day.

"Why don't we start in the back of the class," Miss Jones said, putting back on her oversize glasses, which made her look like a giant bug.

"I'm Billy Robertson. I love history and I was Miss Morris's favorite student." Everyone giggled. Judging by the amount of time he spent in the principal's office, Billy wasn't any teacher's favorite student.

When it finally came around to her turn, Louise lost her nerve. "My name is Louise Lambert and I'm on the swim team," she said quickly, her cheeks burning hot. It was true she was a good swimmer, but that wasn't really the defining thing about her. Louise looked down at a pencil sketch of a Grecian-style dress she had absentmindedly drawn on a blank page in her notebook. Why was she unable to admit that she liked vintage clothing? She couldn't be the only one who was afraid of being a little different, afraid of Billy making one of his trademark mean comments from the back of the room. But it felt that way. Moments like that made her realize her self-confidence was hanging on by a thread.

After the whole class had taken turns and told some inane half truth (or flat-out lie), Miss Jones looked up at the large clock above her desk.

"Well, I guess we still have time to begin the movie. As the school year is almost over, I am going to start prepping you for next year's social studies curriculum, where you will learn about ancient civilizations. I thought we would start with one of the greatest epics of all time. Can someone get the lights, please?"

The fluorescent lights snapped off, and Miss Jones wheeled a squeaky television cart to the front of the room. The blue screen sent an eerie glow throughout the classroom. "How do these things work?" she mumbled under her breath as she fiddled with the old DVD player. "Can someone give me a hand?" No one moved. *"Anyone?"* Bethany MacMillan reluctantly got up from her seat in the front row and pressed play, and the screen went black.

The sound of a grand marching orchestral score filled the now quiet classroom as the movie opened with black block-letter credits, which Louise knew was what films used in the old days.

"Is it over already?" she heard Billy snicker.

Louise got excited as she saw the names of some of her favorite Old Hollywood stars flash up on the screen. *Elizabeth Taylor, Richard Burton...Directed by Joseph L. Mankiewicz,*

Costumes designed by Irene Sharaff. Louise wrote Irene's name down in her notebook—she'd probably want to Google her later. If this movie was anything like the ones she'd watched with her mom, the costumes were going to be amazing!

Eventually, as the camera panned over remnants of a battle scene, the music was replaced with the deep booming voice of a narrator announcing the triumph of Caesar. Thousands of extras with towering plumes protruding from their bronze helmets brandished swords and were dressed in armor over red-and-brown military uniforms that looked like kilts. "Nice skirts!" Billy shouted at the screen, and before they had so much as glimpsed Elizabeth Taylor, the school bell rang to signal the end of class.

"Read Chapter Eleven in your textbook for tomorrow, please!" the frazzled substitute yelled as the class rushed for the door. "And you should know that I am not averse to pop quizzes!" No one slowed down. They had a sub who was about to show them an *epic* movie that could take them through the remainder of June in school movie time. To Louise, who loved classic movies anyway, the end of the school year just got a whole lot better.

CHAPTER 5

That night, when Louise returned home from swim practice, which was remarkably less fun without her best friend there to crack jokes between the long, exhausting sets, she immediately ran up to her walk-in closet to check that she hadn't made up the whole thing in her head. These days she wasn't sure what was real—she needed to see the physical evidence again with her own chlorine-irritated eyes. She opened the creaky old trunk, tossed her secret stash of Barbie and Ken dolls onto the hardwood floor, and pulled out the poodle necklace. The black metal charm was still cold and very real. Clasping it around her neck, she noticed that the pendant felt strangely warm and comfortable on her chest, as though it had been there all her life. Amazed, she once again examined the antique photograph of Mrs. Lambert that was curling at the edges. She needed to talk to her mom about this, stat. Wearing the necklace over her pale green polyester dress, her curly brown hair still damp and tied back in a bun, Louise headed downstairs for supper. Whatever her dad was cooking smelled so mouth-wateringly delicious she almost couldn't believe she was in her own house.

Mrs. Lambert, looking perfectly poised in a cornflower blue cashmere sweater set, was already sitting in her usual seat at the long mahogany dining table, while Louise's father, again wearing the starched white apron from breakfast, now over a striped button-down shirt with the sleeves pushed up to his elbows, bustled in and out of the kitchen. A crispy roasted chicken was proudly displayed in the center of the table. Louise fingered the poodle necklace nervously, unsure of how her mom would react to her new accessory.

"Dad, this smells amazing."

"Thanks, chicken," he said. "A chicken for my chicken," he teased, setting a platter of rosemary potatoes on the table and giving her a kiss on the top of her drying and frizzing hair.

"Any luck on the job front?" Louise's mother asked Mr. Lambert nervously.

"How could I possibly cook supper and look for a job at the same time?" he responded, winking at his daughter. "And I kind of like this Mr. Mom business. I think I could get used to this."

Her mother half smiled and clutched the strand of pearls tautly around her neck, one of her many nervous habits. "How was school today? I saw you missed the bus," she said, turning toward Louise. Her eyes dropped down to Louise's throat, and her face turned a pale white. "Where...where did you get that?" she stammered.

"Do you like it? Is it yours? I found it in your old steamer trunk with my Barbies. Is it okay if I wear it?" The string of questions tumbled out of Louise's lips.

Mrs. Lambert opened her mouth as if to respond, but no sound came out. Her distracted, faraway look masked whatever was going on right below the surface. "I...I suddenly have a headache," she eventually replied. "I'm sorry, but I'm not hungry. I think I need a rest." She shakily stood up from her high-back chair and placed her unfolded ivory linen napkin on her empty Wedgwood china plate. Without another word, she walked out of the dining room as though in a trance, leaving Louise and a befuddled Mr. Lambert alone with an untouched and perfectly roasted chicken.

CHAPTER 6

The next morning, Mrs. Lambert was out of the house again before Louise sat down to another gourmet breakfast, this time of challah French toast with fresh berries, enthusiastically prepared by her attorney father turned Iron Chef. It was starting to feel as if her own mother was avoiding her.

"Where's Mom?" Louise called over to her dad, who was cleaning the griddle.

"She went shopping. The Pattersons are having a dinner party next week to welcome the Moreau family to Fairview and introduce them to a few local folks, us included," her dad explained as she speared a juicy blackberry and popped it into her mouth. "I think their son Peter is in your school. It's a dress-up event, and I know you like that sort of thing."

"Ooh, I do," Louise said with her mouth full, excited that she had another Fashionista Sale coming up. That would be the perfect place to find a dress!

"Your mother decided to get an early start since I'm home now to get you off to school. And I was given explicit instructions as to what time the bus leaves, so you best be on your way," her dad said, grabbing her syrupy plate and shooing her to the door. "Have a good day at school! I have a pork tenderloin to tackle." Louise noticed a gross slab of raw meat on the counter as she ran out of the kitchen to catch the school bus.

"Brooke, do you want to come?" Louise asked, handing her best friend the embossed lemon yellow stationery with the Fashionista Sale details, which she pulled out of the front pocket of her scuffed-up backpack. They were sitting in their usual seat on the bus, third from the front on the left.

"Sorry, Lou. Kip and I have plans on Saturday," Brooke said, briefly glancing down at the invite before going back to her science textbook. She was always scrambling to finish up the last of her homework assignments during the fifteen-minute ride to school, and Louise was accustomed to supplying her friend with some of the answers. "I promised him I'd go to his lacrosse game."

"You're choosing a boy? Over *moi*?" Louise asked pointedly, raising her eyebrows in mock surprise.

"It's not like that. I mean, you didn't even invite me the

last time—your mom had to tell me where you were! I guess I should feel privileged that you even want me to come."

Louise turned away and looked out the dirty, streaked bus window. Sometimes a few sarcastic words from her best friend were more painful than a whole year of Billy Robertson's teasing. Not that it was an either/or situation. As if on cue, Billy popped up in the seat behind them as though he had been waiting for his opportunity to butt in.

"Nice dress, Louise. When did they make that one, 1950?" he asked, cracking up. Louise protectively wrapped her favorite navy cardigan around her blue-and-red plaid minidress with the white butterfly collar, which she thought looked like something a librarian from the sixties would wear—but in a good way. Leave it to Billy to make her feel embarrassed by one of her favorite vintage outfits. "Is that, like, a Salvation Army special?" he continued, refusing to let up until he got some sort of reaction from them.

"Ugh, get a life," Brooke said, rolling her eyes at Billy. "Go back to whatever cave you crawled out of and leave us alone. Louise, have I mentioned how much I *love* your dress?" Her friend always confidently stood up for her when Louise just wanted to slink under the seat and hide. Then, sensing Louise's dejection and returning to their previous topic of conversation, Brooke asked, "Can I bring Kip?"

35

"No," Louise answered quickly. The Fashionista Sale was private. If anyone else from her school knew about it, she felt as if the magic would be ruined. And that Marla and Glenda might never come back to Fairview.

"Okay, fine, I'll meet you there after the game. Don't forget to text me the address. And, Lou, please try not to contract any food poisoning or get a concussion before I get there," Brooke joked. Each time Louise had visited the Fashionista Sale, she seemed to have some unfortunate and potentially life-threatening incident occur. In more ways than her friend even realized. But considering the amazing adventures she'd had, not to mention the most unbelievable selection of vintage clothing she had ever encountered, going again was totally worth the risk.

The girls had shared and overanalyzed every minuscule detail of their lives up until this point, but when she had tried to show Brooke a photo taken on the A deck of the *Titanic* of her with the Astors, her friend just grinned and nodded as though she were humoring a mental patient. So what if the photo was a little blurry—Louise knew it really was her. And after her decadent and dangerous time hanging out with Marie Antoinette during prerevolutionary France, Louise decided it was best to keep the unbelievable stories to herself for now. The only person who could understand was Stella, which was exactly why Louise needed to find her again. Louise had first encountered her fellow Fashionista in the body of Adelaide, the portly daughter of King Louis XV, who had acted strangely suspicious of her. But after she'd caught a glimpse of "Adelaide" in the palace's Hall of Mirrors, Louise had discovered she was actually an eighth-grade girl from Manhattan with pink elastics on her braces! Stella was the only person who knew what Louise was going through.

"I'll try," Louise said, smiling. "Thanks."

"Of course." Brooke gave her friend a reassuring look. "That's what friends are for," she sang as the bus pulled into the manicured circular driveway of Fairview Junior High, dropping them off for another humdrum day of school.

CHAPTER 7

Later that night, over the perfectly cooked pork with home-made applesauce that Mr. Lambert had been slaving over all day, Louise once again tried to broach the subject of the poodle necklace.

"Mom, can you please tell me where you got this neck-lace?" she asked, fingering the charm around her neck, which she had put back on again when she got home from swim practice. "It's, like, vitally important."

"Hmmm..." Mrs. Lambert paused, looking down at her plate as she nibbled on a string bean. "I'm not sure, but I can't wait to show you the dress I bought from Nordstrom for the Pattersons' dinner party. And it was on sale! What are you going to wear, Louise?" her mom asked, completely avoiding the subject. "They had such good deals at the mall. Maybe we should go shopping together."

"I don't know. I thought I could get something at the next Fashionista Sale," Louise replied, hoping to get *some* sort of reaction from her once-again perfectly controlled mother. "There's another one this weekend that I really want to go to." She could have sworn she saw Mrs. Lambert's shoulders tighten just a bit, as though she had a momentary, nearly imperceptible muscle spasm. Her mother's typical faraway gaze seemed to settle on the portrait of Louise's great-aunt Alice Baxter, which hung opposite her on the deep-red walls with the rest of their ancestors, gloomily gazing down at them with their fixed, oil-painted stares. In the painting, her great-aunt must have been at least eighty years old and looked nothing like the gorgeous actress whom Louise had embodied on the *Titanic*. It was hard to believe she was even the same person.

Louise heard Stella's voice replaying in her head: "*Isn't it in your family, too?*" That was it—Stella! Maybe Stella could give her some answers. There actually was another Traveling Fashionista out there, and Louise needed to find her!

"Louise, please don't twirl your hair at the dinner table," her mother finally replied. Louise dropped her hand into her lap midtwirl, not even realizing she was doing it.

"How am I going to find Stella?" Louise asked into her oversize red lip phone.

"That girl I met at the last vintage sale?" Brooke asked.

"Yeah, I have a few questions I was hoping to ask her. About...this thrift shop in New York that I wanted to check out," Louise said, not able to tell her best friend the real truth. "I can't remember the name of it."

"Lou, the rest of us do live in the twenty-first century. Use the Internet. You can find anyone."

"Right, of course." She had kind of fantasized about getting on the Metro North train and heading to Manhattan to track down Stella in person. But she hadn't exactly thought through the part of what would happen once she arrived at Grand Central Terminal.

"Oh, wait, Kip is on the other line. Can you hold on?"

"I'll see you tomorrow. I have some detective work to do anyway," Louise replied, not quite able to hide her annoyed tone. *I better find Stella*, she thought, as her current best friend seemed to be drifting further away from her by the second. She was secretly starting to hate Kip.

As soon as Louise hung up the landline, which her parents insisted she use to prevent too much radiation from entering her ear canal, her cell buzzed with a text message. Maybe Brooke had realized how brushed off Louise was feeling after all. But, surprisingly, it was a text from Todd!

Meet us at food court tmrow?

Louise paused, unsure of what to do.

Why can't you just ask me on a normal date? She wasn't really up for hanging out with Todd and his skater friends, and particularly not Tiff. The insecure voice in her head made her feel silly to have imagined it was even a date in the first place. And she didn't want to be a total hypocrite and miss swim practice after giving Brooke such a hard time yesterday.

She finally responded: **Srry can't make it.**

Todd immediately answered: **:(**

She could not date someone who communicated with emoticons, but still she felt a pang of regret. Maybe she should have said yes. Maybe it would have been fun. But she also wanted to see what happened with Peter. It was probably good to keep her options open for a while anyway.

For once, she had more important things to distract her. Louise opened her computer and Googled "Stella New York City." She got a page of random results: Stella Adler Acting Studio, Stella Bistro, Stella's Pizza, Stella Management Co....Okay, it was time to get a bit more specific. "Stella New York City Vintage Fashionista."

And there it was—Stella had a vintage-fashion blog! *Stella's Vintage Style Files. Of course*, Louise thought, shaking her head. *Why didn't I think of that earlier?* Louise clicked on the "About Me" tab, and a photo popped up of a girl who looked vaguely familiar, wearing a white-and-black tweed vintage Chanel jacket over a white T-shirt, blue sailor jeans, and funky brown leather platform shoes, and smiling a mouthful

of braces. Louise zoomed in—those looked like little pink elastics. This had to be the right Stella!

MY BIO:

I'm a vintage-obsessed fashionista. I love searching through thrift stores for the perfect vintage outfit and getting to experience different histories through clothing—or at least in my imagination.☺

She eagerly started reading Stella's latest post:

Hey, Vintage Fashionistas! Sorry it's been so long since my last post—I guess you could say I was held up in customs from my last trip to Paris, which was inspired by my fixation on all things French—French movies, French music, French boys, and, most importantly, French fashion. From my great-great-aunt twice removed Coco Chanel's awesome quilted bags to Yves Saint Laurent's covetable color-block jersey minidresses, I can never get enough of French style. This photo shoot will let you know where my head (and wardrobe!) was. Bon Voyage!

Louise began clicking through the slide show: Each photo was an image of Stella in some posh New York City apartment posing in different French-themed outfits while eating croissants and macaroons. The last picture showed her sitting at a grand piano wearing a pale pink corseted ball gown with white bows running down the bodice, like something Adelaide could have worn.

My new obsession, the blog continued in the next post down the page, are vintage military jackets. You can wear them casually with skinny jeans or over a thrifted Betsey Johnson baby-doll dress. I am going to test-drive some this week and report back. Stay tuned, fashionistas! XOXO, Stella

Louise immediately subscribed to the blog and sent her a message.

Hey, Stella,

OHMIGOD, can you believe that we met before the French Revolution? I am still recovering from those corsets! Those gowns were ah-mazing, and I kind of miss the croissants as well, but it seems like we escaped Versailles just in time. Where else have you traveled? Maybe we can go vintage shopping together sometime.

Louise paused and reconsidered. What if by some chance this actually wasn't the right Stella? This girl would think she was a total lunatic. Louise deleted the message and thought for a moment about how to word it while still acknowledging their bizarre situation. She decided to take a slightly more subtle approach.

Hey, Stella,

I think we've met in the past! Are you going to the next Fashionista Sale this weekend? Would LOVE to catch up!

Your fellow fashionista,

Louise Lambert, age 12 years, 9 months, 6 days, 4 hours, 10 minutes, and 15 seconds

She impatiently refreshed her computer for the next thirty minutes, hoping for some kind of response from Stella, and then finally, when Louise could barely keep her eyes open for another minute, she shut down her laptop and reluctantly went to bed.

CHAPTER 8

Each morning for the last few days, Mrs. Lambert had already left the house by the time Louise had woken up for school, and she'd somehow managed to change the subject or come down with a migraine every time Louise had attempted to bring up the poodle necklace or Fashionista Sale. Louise still hadn't received an e-mail back from Stella, either, despite checking her Gmail about twenty times a day, and she was starting to feel nervous and insecure that maybe she had made a mistake in trying to contact her after all. When they'd met, Stella had made a point of telling Louise that she was thirteen years old and from New York City, as opposed to Louise, who was only twelve and from the suburbs, but didn't she want to be friends anyway?

Louise reread the folded-up, handwritten note given to her by Marla and Glenda after the last sale: *You have your friends, you have your family, and soon you will have your fellow Fashionistas.*

But what if her own mother was also one of her "fellow Fashionistas"? It seemed as if the only way she was going to get any answers about how her mother tied into all this, and who exactly these other time travelers were, was to go the source—she was going to have to ask Marla and Glenda directly.

The few days leading up to the next Fashionista Vintage Sale that weekend were torture. It was as though time were stretching out like a grilled cheese sandwich. Days felt like weeks, and the week felt like an eternity. The only highlights were that she was getting to watch a classic Elizabeth Taylor and Richard Burton movie in history class and that she had run into Peter a few times in the hallway again. He already seemed to be getting the hang of everything, making new friends with eighth graders whom Louise didn't know. In her seventh-grade insecurity, Louise found herself keeping her distance even though he would smile and wave to her no matter whom he was with. She was really excited about the Pattersons' party next week and getting to spend time with him again outside school, hopefully in a newly acquired vintage dress from the next sale. Maybe she could learn more about the French side of his family. She just needed to make it through the school week.

Finally, the weekend, and the day of the much-obsessed-over Traveling Fashionista Vintage Sale, arrived. Once again, her uncharacteristically absent mother was already out of the house and running errands, so at least, Louise rationalized, she wouldn't have to explain where she was going or worry that her mother would stop her and drag her to the Stamford Mall instead.

She left a note on the pad on the kitchen counter so her parents wouldn't worry.

Dear Mom and Dad,
Going to find a vintage dress for the Pattersons' dinner. Be back soon!
Your only (and favorite) daughter,
Louise Ann Lambert

Grabbing a green apple from the wooden fruit bowl, she texted Brooke the address and took off with her backpack in search of her next exciting experience. On the walk over, Louise double-checked that she was still wearing her mother's necklace and couldn't help but imagine all the possible adventures that could be in store for her. What if she found a pair of bell-bottoms that took her back to Woodstock? Or a Mary Quant dress that would take her to London in the sixties! Or a Versace corset that would take her to a glamorous party in Italy. The possibilities were endless.

She had to be careful with her selection, though. With her

luck, a cute military jacket would place Louise on the front lines of the Revolutionary War, for all she knew! Of course there was always the slight possibility that after her last time at the sale, when she covertly tried on that robin's egg blue ball gown while Marla and Glenda weren't looking, she wouldn't get to experience any more magical incidents after all. The shop owners were none too pleased that Louise had disobeyed their orders and consequently run into another Fashionista in the past, which was apparently against the rules. Not to mention that Louise almost lost her head in eighteenth-century France as a result—literally. She prayed Marla and Glenda weren't the kind of people to hold a grudge. When she turned onto Gates Lane, she swore she felt some wispy fabric brush the back of her neck. But when she reached up, nothing was there except for the clasp of her necklace. It was probably a breeze.

Before she knew it, Louise had arrived. 303 GATES LANE. This had to be the place! She lived only a few streets away from here and had decided to walk instead of taking her bike. It was so close, and she didn't want to risk another concussion from her clumsy riding. Louise stood in front of the deserted warehouse and triple-checked her invite. *Weird.*

It was funny how once Marla and Glenda discovered an address, it became exotic, but before Louise received the invitation, 303 Gates Lane had been just another boring one-story sprawling industrial complex on a typical Fairview street. She wouldn't have looked twice at it, and, in fact, up until this day she hadn't. They were continuing to make her see her small suburban town in a new and more enchanting light. She quickly walked across the deserted asphalt parking lot toward the main entrance, which had 303 stenciled in black numbers on the steel door. When she was only a few feet away, she felt an intense heat on her chest, as if the charm necklace she was wearing were burning. Then, almost as quickly as she had noticed it, the sensation went away. No sooner had she reached for the handle than the door flung open and a startled Louise was yanked across the threshold.

CHAPTER 9

"Marla! She's baaack!" a familiar voice sang.

"Fabulous, oh, this is simply mah-velous. We hoped a little guillotine wouldn't scare you away from your destiny."

A rather glamorous-looking Marla and Glenda immediately wrapped a neon green feather boa around Louise's shoulders and hooked her into the shop. To Louise's great relief, it seemed that all had been forgiven.

"And where's your little blonde friend?" Glenda asked, poking her head of red hair out into the blinding sunshine, searching the empty lot for Brooke. "I suppose she'll pop in later. We've grown quite fond of her as well." She slammed the door firmly behind her. Louise squeezed her eyes shut, willing them to adjust to the dimly lit store.

"She said she'd meet me here. She's hanging out with her new boyfriend," Louise replied sadly. "Who knows if she'll even show up."

Marla and Glenda shrugged, each throwing an encouraging arm around Louise and guiding her into the newest version of their lively vintage shop. "That happens to the best of 'em. Trust us—she'll be back," Marla said.

Louise spun around in awe, trying to take everything in. She was once again overwhelmed by the sheer magnitude of *stuff*. It was like the inside of her school locker taken to the nth degree. The sprawling, loftlike room had some of the same furniture as the previous sales: the ivory-colored wooden armoire and shabbily upholstered chaises with the springs poking out, even the old-fashioned dusty Victrola now pushed into the far corner, which was emitting scratchy piano music that sounded like a score of a silent Charlie Chaplin movie. There was definitely a Hollywood theme going on in the shop. She paused to check out framed black-and-white posters from classic films such as *Casablanca* and *Breakfast at Tiffany's*, which were hung slightly askew on the roughly plastered white walls. She wanted to get one of those for her bedroom. The store now looked like how she'd imagine the wardrobe department of an old movie studio to be.

Marla and Glenda were wearing pink feather boas, with matching tortoiseshell, cat-eye sunglasses shading their iridescent green eyes, and looking pretty fabulous themselves compared with their usual drab black wool dresses. Marla was caked in heavy stage makeup, with a thick coat of powder and foundation almost masking the wart that was still slightly detectable on the tip of her pointy nose. Her chin hairs had been plucked, save for one lone straggler that remained on the left side of her lower lip. When Marla smiled, Louise could see that the bright red lipstick she was wearing was smudged across her two front teeth.

Glenda, whose towering height never stopped her from wearing high-heeled shoes, was decked out in a knee-length black sequined cocktail dress. Her flame red hair was done up in a fifties-style beehive that barely moved because of what must have been an obscene amount of hair spray. To Louise, who wasn't even five feet tall, Glenda looked like a stylish giant. On their necks were the heavy gold chains with black poodle charms that looked exactly like the necklace her mother owned, which she now wore.

Louise pulled the necklace out from underneath her Laura Ashley blue paisley sundress, hoping to shock *them* for a change. The women glanced down at her throat and let out a long, deep laugh as though they were expecting this. "Welcome to the club, dahling. Our Fashionistas always did know how to accessorize!"

Louise swallowed her surprise at their casual reaction as they eagerly led her around the store, excitedly grabbing vintage clothes for her approval: plaid polyester bell-bottom pants that were strewn on a canvas director's chair, a bohemian floral Chloé dress from the seventies, a Hattie Carnegie tailored suit, an Elsa Schiaparelli trademark pink hat in the shape of a shoe. Louise picked up the shoe-shaped hat in awe. She would be too shy to wear something like this, but it was awesome.

"You know, when Elsa was your age, she thought she was so ugly that she tried to plant seeds on her face and in her ears so that beauty could grow," Marla said.

"Really?" Louise asked, surprised. She thought someone who made such bold pieces had to have been born confident.

"Yes, isn't that such a sad story? What girl doesn't think she's beautiful?" Marla asked as a lone tear streaked down her makeup-spackled face.

"Sometimes I can relate," Louise replied, putting the hat on her frizzy brown head. Marla couldn't help but smile— after all, Louise had a shocking pink shoe on her head. It was hard to be sad when you looked so silly.

Signed and framed portraits of movie stars posing with Glenda and Marla hung in clusters on the wall. Piles of yellowing and curled movie scripts on the floor served as pedestals for worn leather tap shoes that looked as if they were from the Jazz Age.

Louise looked down and saw that there were stars on the floor like on the Hollywood Walk of Fame. She saw Audrey Hepburn, Marilyn Monroe, Elizabeth Taylor, Cary Grant, Marlon Brando...all of Louise's and her mother's favorite actors from bygone eras. She wished her mother were here now with her so that they could share this experience. She had inherited her mother's love for old movies—one of their favorite traditions was making popcorn on the stove with lots of butter and watching classic films. And now it seemed that maybe she had inherited a lot more than that.

Louise noticed that one of the photos on the wall was of a young version of her great-aunt Alice Baxter, looking exactly as she remembered her from the photo she saw on the vanity table on the *Titanic* during her first adventure. So they did know her after all! It was signed with a red lipstick smooch: *To Marla and Glenda, Kiss kiss, Alice Baxter.*

"You do know Miss Baxter!" Louise exclaimed.

"Now what are you searching for this time, dahling?" Glenda called from the other side of the room, her voice muffled as her head was stuck inside a large blond-oak wardrobe. She pulled out the same leopard-print coat she'd searched for the last time Louise saw her and triumphantly put it on over her black sequined dress. "How on earth did it get in here?" she muttered.

"How do you know Miss Baxter?" Louise repeated.

"As I've said before, we've worked with the best, and we know 'em all. Now, how can we help you today?" Glenda asked, modeling her coat with a dramatic twirl.

"Don't you usually tell me that?" Louise asked jokingly,

remembering that the last times she was at the store, they seemed to know exactly what she was looking for before she had mentioned her upcoming school dance or fancy-dress birthday party.

"Isn't it time you start figuring that out for yourself?" Marla asked, tying a yellow Hermès silk scarf around her neck with a flourish.

"Well, there's this dinner party at the Pattersons' house that I'm going to with my parents," Louise said pointedly. "I'm supposed to dress up."

"Ooh, we do enjoy a good dinner party! And I think we know just what your mother would love to see you in!" Marla exclaimed with a twinkle in her eye.

"You do? How?" Louise asked, hoping that she would finally get the information she had been searching for.

"Well, we did meet her that time at your house after your slight bout of food poisoning," Glenda said quickly.

"That was not food poisoning! She had the flu!" Marla insisted, looking hurt. "My cooking has never poisoned anyone. That I know of. Although we haven't seen that freckle-faced girl for a while now." Louise's hazel eyes grew wide. "Just kidding, dahling."

"Well, I do have some unanswered questions regarding my mother," Louise cut in, hoping she could get a little more info about how her mom fit into this equation. "I wouldn't mind a few answers. You see, I found—"

"Answers? Isn't that what you go to that dull little school for?" Glenda interrupted.

"You've become so conventional! How about a Valentino instead?" Marla asked suddenly, holding up a gorgeous black tulle Valentino gown with white piping that appeared seemingly out of thin air.

"All the big starlets are dying to wear his dresses, you know." Glenda tossed her pink feather boa dramatically over her shoulder. "Lucky you, sweet pea," she rasped.

Marla threw the Valentino over a flickering floor lamp and took Louise by the arm. "Never mind, that one's been done. I have just the dress for this marvelous little dinner party of yours. Come with me. This one is going to take you to the stars!"

CHAPTER 10

"Now, why don't you try this one on for size, dahling?" Marla asked proudly, pulling out a gorgeous Grecian-style one-shoulder lavender silk and chiffon dress from an open chest of drawers for Louise's approval. The elegantly pleated and fitted bodice had a dramatic single shoulder strap and a wispy, flowing long skirt that fell to the floor. It was old-school glamorous and looked like a variation of a gown she had seen before going down the red carpet of the Oscars or something.

"Ohmigod, I love it!" Louise declared. "It's perfect." She wished she could model it for Brooke. Louise had a feeling that even her friend, despite her lack of enthusiasm for vintage, would admit it was pretty awesome.

"We thought you might," Marla said, beaming. "And, just a hunch, I think your dear mother will also approve. It's classic, timeless, elegant, just like her."

Just as Louise was about to ask her how exactly she knew so

much about her mom, Glenda interrupted. "But we do have so much new inventory! Why don't you browse, take your time, and have a look around before making any final...decisions. A new dress is a big commitment, as I'm sure you've discovered. The wrong selection could completely change the course of your evening."

"And perhaps even more than that." Marla giggled.

"Umm, okay. I guess," Louise said, poking through the racks of clothes, pausing to check out an incredible Prada A-line skirt layered with plastic baubles, but still not able to stop thinking about the pale purple gown she had just been shown. That had to be the one! She had felt that prickly feeling on her arms that told her it was special.

"And we haven't even offered you a snack! Sometimes we get so distracted by fashion that we completely forget our manners," Marla apologized, producing a plate of grayish-looking shrimp cocktail from a small broom closet.

"I think I'll pass," Louise said firmly. *Gross. How long had it been sitting in there?* It could be from the eighties, for all she knew.

"Suit yourself," Marla said with a shrug as she popped a floppy jumbo shrimp into her mouth and swallowed it in one large gulp, tail and all.

Just then, Louise's phone vibrated, and she saw that she had a text from Brooke. **Srry, running LATE!! XO**

Frustrated, Louise turned off her phone and shoved it back into her bag without responding. She felt as though her own friend didn't even want to hang out with her anymore. Brooke would obviously rather be with Kip than the friend she grew up with her whole life. "I'd like to try on that dress now, please. My best friend seems to have abandoned me, so I guess I'll have to make this decision without her."

"Very well. As you'd like it," Marla replied, sliding the appetizer platter beneath a love seat and tossing the dress to Louise, the purple silk train making a graceful sweeping arc across the shop.

"The fitting rooms are in the rear. And we do hope it fits, dahling," Glenda said in her low, raspy drawl. "You never know with vintage. Sometimes something that looks perfectly suited for you on the hanger doesn't work quite as well once you have it on."

Excited, Louise stepped into the makeshift changing room, pulling the tattered red velvet fabric as securely closed behind her as possible. It felt like being behind a stage curtain, as if Louise were changing for a performance or something, and maybe in a way she was. Taped on the full-length dressing room mirror was a black-and-white portrait of a young, gorgeous Marilyn Monroe wearing a skintight, long white sequined dress. She smiled, thinking how much it reminded her of her own mirror back home. She studied herself in comparison with this flawless-looking actress and found it kind of disheartening. But seeing all the movie posters, the stars on the floor, the backstage photos, it felt as though they must be clues for her next adventure. Maybe Louise was going to Hollywood!

She eagerly kicked off her neon pink Converse and yanked her cotton Laura Ashley dress over her head. She tried to immerse herself in the experience, carefully undoing the heavy zipper and clasp, appreciating the luxurious feel of the cool, silk-lined fabric, letting herself get lost in the fantasy and endless possibility she felt as a little kid playing dress-up in her mother's closet. A shiver shot through her when she pushed her arms up through the body of the dress. The dressing room suddenly felt as if it were spinning in fast, tight circles like the Mad Tea Party ride at Disney World.

"*Bon voyage*, dahling! Do report back!" She heard Glenda's husky voice and Marla's chuckle echoing inside her head as she collapsed to the floor in one dramatic fell swoop. Louise definitely knew how to make an exit.

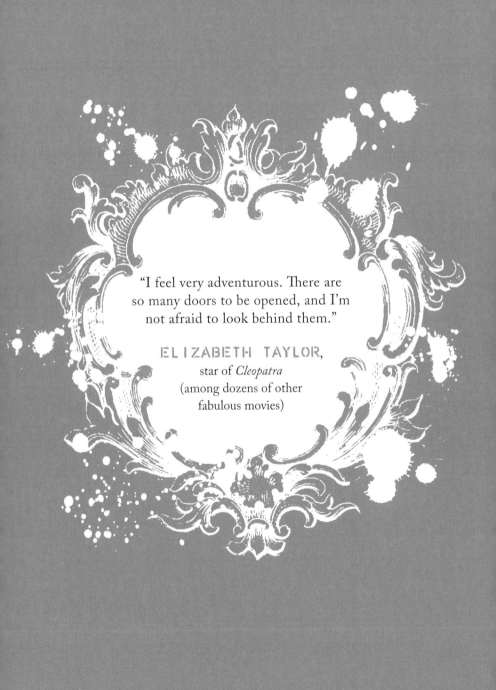

"I feel very adventurous. There are so many doors to be opened, and I'm not afraid to look behind them."

ELIZABETH TAYLOR,
star of *Cleopatra*
(among dozens of other
fabulous movies)

CHAPTER 11

Louise woke up coughing, facedown in a swirling cloud of red dust. Armor-clad men with bronze breastplates and pleated kilts were swarming around her, their dirty leather boots coming alarmingly close to stepping on her head. She immediately felt panic rising up in her throat. *Where am I?* Before she had a moment to get her bearings, Louise felt the ground tremble beneath her hands, and she heard a loud rumbling. To her horror, a large horse-drawn chariot was barreling straight for her! Louise felt a strong grip on her upper arm as someone dragged her out of the dirt road. She screamed, barely avoiding being crushed under the huge wooden wheels as a team of muscular horses sped past. Dazed, she looked up at the boy who had just rescued her. Wearing a kilt and a bronze breastplate of armor, he was around her age and seemed too young to already be a soldier.

"Thanks," Louise gasped. "You just saved my life."

"You should be more careful next time," he said, leading her out of the road. "We're already a year behind schedule. We don't need anyone getting killed by a horse."

"Sorry," Louise said, not exactly sure what she was apologizing for. *What kind of schedule?* Louise wondered. The young soldier helped ease her down onto a low stone step, where she caught her breath and leaned back, trying to soak in the unfamiliar surroundings. It was as though she had woken up in the middle of a battle. *Am I at war?* A group of men carrying scuffed bronze shields strolled by leisurely.

"C'mon, Jack," one of the men called to the boy. "The maestro has requested our presence in the battlefield."

"Are you sure you're all right?" the boy named Jack asked, giving Louise a curious and slightly concerned look. She nodded, still in a state of shock, and then he left her with one last backward glance to go join the rest of the soldiers. The men were laughing and seemed to be in no rush to get to whatever fight they were headed to. She thought she heard one of them say he wanted a pizza, but that couldn't be right. It seemed unlikely that Domino's would deliver to a location like this!

Louise looked down to see that she was still wearing her lavender chiffon silk dress, only now it was covered in rust-colored dust. She didn't seem to be in any immediate danger, and her initial fear subsided. Louise tried to brush off the bits of dirt that clung to the silk fabric and make herself look a bit more presentable while she figured out what exactly she was supposed to be doing, and where on earth she was.

Glancing up, she realized that she was sitting on the bottom step of an enormous, towering pyramid, like the ones she had seen in books about ancient Egypt. These were definitely olden times, like really old. This dress wasn't vintage; it was prehistoric! She was going to kill Marla and Glenda. Maybe this was their way of getting back at her for traveling to Versailles without their approval! Some kind of cruel joke or lesson—like how superconfident, gorgeous Stella ended up in the old, curmudgeonly body of Adelaide. But how was it possible for a garment to survive thousands of years and still be in such good condition? It didn't make any sense. And despite the fact that the sun was directly overhead without a cloud in the sky, it wasn't as hot as Louise had imagined the desert would be. In fact, it was pretty much the perfect temperature, seventy-five with no humidity. Maybe it was winter or something.

"There you are!" exclaimed a blue-eyed, freckly girl wearing a simple white toga. She grabbed Louise by the hand. "What happened to you?"

"I think I was almost crushed by a chariot," Louise said.

"Whoa, crazy. Are you okay?" she asked, but continued on without giving Louise a chance to answer. "You'll never guess what I just saw! Apparently all the rumors are true!"

71

The girl talked as though she and Louise were good friends and they were picking up on a conversation they'd started moments ago.

"What rumors?" Louise asked.

"Come with me. You're never going to believe this," the girl instructed, dragging Louise through the soft, warm sand, which kept getting into her sandals as she tried to keep up. The desert landscape was dotted with palm trees, and the girl stopped short and pointed to one particularly thick trunk. Louise couldn't make out any faces, but she saw a woman in a periwinkle blue dress talking closely behind the tree with a man who must have been an army general.

"I saw them kissing," the girl explained, wide-eyed when Louise didn't respond. "I mean anyone could—it's the middle of the day! Don't you think they're taking this a little too far? Oh no, they're looking this way. If they spot us, we could be canned!"

"Taking what too far?" Louise asked as the girl quickly pulled her away from the tree.

"Don't play innocent," she said, rolling her eyes. "I need to get back to my mark," she called, taking off through the desert. "See you tonight!"

Louise, alone and now more confused than ever, headed back to where she started to try to get her bearings. She turned right behind the "pyramid" and was surprised to discover that it wasn't a pyramid at all—it was actually a two-dimensional facade! The backside was constructed of cheap-looking plywood and propped up by unfinished crossbeams. Louise wasn't in ancient Egypt after all; she was on a film set! Men dressed in button-down shirts and carrying megaphones and clipboards were leaning against the wood and chatting in groups with some of the armored men she had seen before, including Jack, who was now devouring a slice of pepperoni pizza. She almost tripped over a roll of cable that was connected to a giant lighting rig and barely avoided wiping out in front of a particularly cute "soldier" wearing a red cape.

"Careful," her rescuer warned as she tried unsuccessfully to hide her stumble by breaking into a slight jog. "You really are accident-prone, aren't you?"

"I guess," she said, blushing. No matter what year it was and how glamorous her surroundings, Louise still managed to display her trademark klutziness. Embarrassed, she quickly walked around to the other side of the set and noticed a camera on a rigged track. A man wearing a tweed coat and a tie who must have been the director looked into the lens while smoking a pipe.

"I need Caesar, I mean Rex, to walk down these steps and address the army when he gets to the third one," he boomed as a blond man in a navy blazer ran over to the pyramid and put a strip of white tape on the designated step.

"Is this good, Joe?" he asked.

"Fine. Now let's get this show on the road. The studio will have my hide if we don't get this scene finished by nightfall. Where is Miss Taylor? She's up next. Let's get her in wardrobe immediately. I don't want to be waiting around all afternoon like yesterday."

"Ummm..." There was a long, uncomfortable pause from the blond in the blazer. "We don't know where she is, sir."

"You don't know?" Joe repeated angrily. The stocky director massaged his temples with his index fingers as though the news gave him an instant migraine. His wide forehead creased with wrinkles. Strangely, even though it was sunny and warm, he was wearing white cotton gloves. His dark brown hair was receding, and the bald patch at the top of his head was beaded with sweat.

"She disappeared about an hour ago," the man in the sport coat replied nervously.

"She what? You are telling me the most famous movie actress in the world...disappeared?"

"Yes, sir," he said in an even quieter voice.

"I haven't slept in about six months rewriting this doggone picture. My nerves are completely shot. Are you, young man, trying to kill me?" The extremely agitated director's veins were now bulging out of his neck, and his face had turned an unnatural shade of purple.

"No, sir," he whispered.

"Well, she's got to be here somewhere. For the *one million dollars* the studio is paying her, she had better be around here somewhere. Maybe her costar will know where she is. Someone get Richard! Check her hotel. Check the spa. I don't care what you have to do—*find her!*" the director yelled as the blond man ran off in the opposite direction, pushing past the throng of uniformed soldiers, who tried to jump out of his way.

Louise looked around at all the thousands of heavily armored centurions who were totally intimidating only a few moments ago and realized they must all be just extras wearing costumes. And then she had an even more amazing realization.

"Joan, there you are! Irene has been looking everywhere for you. Where have you been?" Louise's racing mind was interrupted by a harried young man with round black-rimmed glasses and a clipboard who began pulling her by the arm. "And what exactly happened to you? Why are you wearing one of the costumes? More important, why is it so dirty? Did Mr. Mankiewicz ask you to stand in for one of the actresses again?" he asked, looking her over with a perplexed expression.

"I guess so. Who are you?" Louise couldn't help but ask.

"Sorry, I suppose we haven't been formally introduced yet," he said, pushing his glasses up on his nose, which was dotted with beads of sweat, and offering Louise his hand after wiping it on his chino pants. "I'm Howie Sanders. I just started as a production assistant last week when the last guy quit. And I'm going to get into a heap of trouble if you don't get back into the wardrobe tent."

"Sorry, Howie. I guess I got a little distracted."

"I'd say. You might want to get yourself together. You have a fitting with Miss Taylor in ten minutes," he said, flipping through some pages on his clipboard and cross-checking it with his Timex. Yup, Louise was pretty sure they didn't make those in ancient Egypt.

Louise smoothed out her dress and retied her hair into a tight bun. In Hollywood, "Miss Taylor" could refer to only one extremely famous and glamorous person. If this missing actress was who she thought she was, Louise was quite possibly about to meet one of her all-time film idols, Dame Elizabeth Taylor, in person! "I'm ready. Thanks for finding me, Howie. And don't worry, I think Miss Taylor is running a little bit late herself."

Louise's predicament just got a whole lot more fabulous!

CHAPTER 12

Louise ran to keep up with Howie, who was rushing ahead of her, while still trying to take in as much of her first Hollywood movie experience as possible. Compared with being a passenger on a sinking ship or a lady of a French royal court that was about to be overthrown in a bloody revolution, Louise had totally hit the fashion jackpot with this adventure! It was as if she had stepped across the screen into one of her and her mother's favorite movies. Louise had actually made it to the Golden Age of Hollywood!

"Who's that?" Louise asked as a woman hurried by, her face partially obscured by a towering stack of papers.

"That's Elaine, the script supervisor," he replied over his shoulder without slowing down. "With all the revisions and changes they've made to this picture, she just might have the hardest job on set."

Louise took in a whiff of cooked bacon as they sped by a

tent full of long tables covered in white tablecloths and sur-rounded by folding chairs. It was packed with actresses wear-ing lots of makeup and multicolored togas with white fuzzy slippers, chatting and laughing while drinking coffee out of paper cups. She kept nearly tripping over the ground, which was booby-trapped with wires and extension cords to keep the large lights and fans running.

They passed a group of trailers with names written in black uppercase letters on gold stars tacked to each door. REX was on one, RICHARD on another, but the largest, double-wide trailer was designated LIZ. The man she had seen before in the navy sport coat was sitting on the steps to the missing actress's door, his blond head in his hands. From the looks of his slumped posture, it did not look as though his search had been successful.

Suddenly, the door to Rex's trailer flung open and a tall man in a maroon cloak with a gold wreath in his salt-and-pepper hair stormed out. A flustered woman dressed like a secretary from *Mad Men* trailed behind him.

"Mr. Harrison, please, Mr. Mankiewicz needs you at the base of the pyramid steps. This is your big scene!"

"Call me Caesar!" he projected in a booming British accent as though he were delivering a soliloquy to an audience from the stage.

"Yes, Caesar, please come with me to the set," the woman pleaded.

"I will not utter another line until my agent has it in writing that Richard and I have equal billing. If Marc Antony is on a poster, Caesar should be on the same poster!"

"I'm sure that can be arranged, Rex, I mean, Caesar." The woman was now near tears. "Please do this one scene and we can iron out all the details later."

He looked strangely familiar, and then Louise remembered that, for one, she had just been watching this exact movie in history class, but also that he played Henry Higgins in *My Fair Lady*! She and her mom loved that movie. She was about to tell him that when he briskly walked past, and then she realized that maybe he hadn't made that film yet. And besides, Henry Higgins was turning out to be a bit of a jerk in real life.

"Here we are! Costumes!" Louise and Howie stopped abruptly in front of a large tent covered with a dusty red awning.

"I'll leave you here. I need to report back to Walter, my boss. Good luck! Pleasure officially meeting you," Howie added before adjusting his glasses once more and running off in the opposite direction.

Louise lifted the heavy tent flap and stepped inside. She broke into a huge grin; she had just arrived in fashion heaven.

The wardrobe area was almost as crazy and bustling as Marla and Glenda's Fashionista shop. Rolling racks of costumes for men, women, kids, and even horses were crammed under the canvas canopy. A haphazard pile of engraved bronze shields and swords was in the middle of the floor. A row of worn, lace-up brown leather boots and gladiator sandals in every possible size ran along one side of the tent.

There was a whole colorful rack marked ELIZABETH crammed full with long silk and floor-sweeping linen gowns of periwinkle blue, burnt sienna, white and gold, and forest green, many of which she recognized from the film. Louise couldn't help but run her hand along the endless row of luxurious fabrics, savoring the feel of the wispy material tickling her palm. A long folding table was covered in a line of mannequin heads donning dark braided wigs; elaborate headdresses with ostrich plumes and feathers; and heaps of gold jewelry, cuffs, collar necklaces studded with deep red garnet and golden yellow topaz, and dangling emerald and ruby earrings. Louise was entranced in a state of pure Fashionista bliss! *People actually did this? Like, for a job?* Maybe if she became a costume designer when she grew up, she could hang out with movie stars and play dress-up her whole life after all. Quite possibly, Louise had not just found the wardrobe tent, she had also found her calling.

"Joan! I need a hand here. Where the heavens have you

been? And what happened to you?" a sharp, angry voice broke her out of her reverie. This woman must be Irene Sharaff, the costume designer for the movie *Cleopatra* and, it seemed, Louise's new boss. And she did not seem pleased *at all*.

"Umm..." Louise stuttered.

"And take that costume off! You'd think they'd have enough extras without poaching my staff!"

"Well, I..."

"Never mind, I don't have time!" Irene must have been around her mother's age, with thick dark hair that was fastened in a giant chignon at the top of her head and deep brown eyes lined in heavy pencil, accentuated by a strong nose and a sharp chin. A perfectly round beauty mark dotted the right side of her eyebrow. She was wearing a simple black knee-length pencil skirt with a tucked crisp white blouse, looking more like a teacher from the sixties than a fashion plate. But in her hands was the most marvelous sunset orange silk, pleated dress Louise had ever seen.

"Ooh, that's beautiful," Louise gushed.

"We just got this magnificent imported silk delivered, and I sewed it this morning. I think it will be perfect for the Roman gala scene, don't you?"

"Yes, it's perfect!" Louise exclaimed with the foresight of someone who had just watched that exact scene in class the day before.

"I do hope it fits her. Judy was difficult, but in all my years of costume design, I have never experienced anything quite like this."

"Judy?" Louise asked.

"Judy Garland, of course," Irene responded. Whoa, this woman had worked with Dorothy from *The Wizard of Oz*!

"How can a woman go up or down several sizes in one night? Luckily, the Greek-style gowns are a bit forgiving, but the Egyptian tunics all need to be restitched with every slice of chocolate cake she eats!" Irene exclaimed.

Too bad wrap dresses aren't popular yet, Louise thought. *It would save Irene a lot of work!*

"And all the weight she lost after that last hospitalization! I've never heard of anyone going to the hospital as much as she does. No one in the audience will even believe it's the same Cleopatra—she looks so different from day to day!"

"Maybe they can use some special effects or something when they finish," Louise suggested.

"You tell me what kind of special effect will change an actress's weight in a picture," Irene guffawed.

Louise had to bite her tongue to keep from telling her that in a few decades *all* actresses were pretty much retouched to look thinner. They definitely didn't have Photoshop or CGI on this film set.

"What was your favorite production to work on?" Louise

couldn't help but ask. She was currently assisting a costume-design legend—she had a ton of questions.

"Oh, *West Side Story* was fabulous. I absolutely loved making those dresses for darling Natalie Wood! *The King and I* was marvelous as well. I save a little keepsake from each picture to remember it by, maybe a little piece of jewelry or a skirt," Irene continued, her hard features softening as she clutched the orange gown to her chest and dreamily reflected on her past. "It's a way for me to hold on to all the memories. I just don't think I could pick a favorite," she said wistfully. But then, just as quickly, she snapped back to attention. "Although at this point I'd say anything but this picture. I've never had such a large costume budget and such an enormous headache. Which will get even bigger if I don't fix this dress. I need you to find that gold belt with the tassels for me. We need it for the next scene, and Liz will be here any minute," Irene said briskly, signaling that their brief bonding session had come to an abrupt end. She handed Louise a pile of Joan's clothes for her to change into.

"Sure thing," Louise answered quickly, trying to act like this Joan girl even though she had no idea how to find anything in this crammed space. She ducked behind one of the racks and switched into Joan's white short-sleeved cotton blouse, black capri pants, and loafers. She felt very Audrey Hepburn.

"Any luck?" Irene asked.

"Not yet." She searched the accessories table for the elusive belt but with no success. She didn't want to get fired on her first day! Checking behind one of the racks of long, embroidered gold dresses, Louise came across an old wooden trunk that had a sign written in thick black marker—SOURCE MATERIAL. PRIVATE. KEEP OUT!—tacked onto the top. It might as well have read LOUISE, PLEASE OPEN ME!, as that was her first overwhelming instinct. She looked around to see if she was being watched by her new boss—she wasn't—and carefully lifted the heavy lid of the trunk. *If they actually wanted to keep people away, they would have put a lock on it, right?* she rationalized. And maybe the belt Irene was looking for was in there.

The interior of the trunk smelled like stale mothballs and appeared to be empty, just filled with crumpled newspapers and tissue paper. Louise pulled out a balled-up sheet of newsprint and discovered it was a copy of *Variety* from 1961! Unnerved, she read the top headline: "Production Continues on Jinxed Cleopatra Film: The Most Expensive Movie Ever Made." She flipped open the newspaper and continued reading. "Production has resumed on the epic film *Cleopatra*, which is now considered the most expensive film to date, with an astronomical budget of $44 million. Director Rouben Mamoulian has resigned and was replaced by Academy

Award–winning director Joseph Mankiewicz. Star Elizabeth Taylor, who fell ill at the beginning of production, has recovered from an emergency tracheotomy and is now cleared by her doctors to continue shooting. Rumor has it that Elizabeth and her costar Richard Burton are doing a lot more than just acting on the set, much to the chagrin of their respective spouses. We can only project what calamity will happen next on this seemingly doomed production!" That must have been who that girl was trying to show Louise behind the tree! She had just seen the beginning of one of the greatest and most dramatic Hollywood love stories of all time!

"Joan? The belt, please!" a harried Irene called out to her.

Louise quickly stowed the newspaper back inside the seemingly bare trunk and decided that maybe she wasn't the only one who had ignored the KEEP OUT warning, but then she felt a hard object edged into the corner. Louise eagerly pulled out a huge, single milky pearl on a gold pendant dangling from a thin chain. She had never seen a pearl that ginormous in her life! It was creamy and iridescent, and it practically glowed in her hands. It was the most beautiful necklace she had ever seen. Louise held the chain up to her neck and felt a peculiar warmth on her chest, kind of like how she felt when she put on her mother's poodle charm necklace.

"Ireney!" a strangely familiar voice sang from outside the tent. Louise heard a commotion of people as she turned to

see *the* Elizabeth Taylor storm into the wardrobe department wearing a low-cut periwinkle blue sleeveless gown and dramatic matching blue eye shadow with thick cat-eye black liner that highlighted her lavender-colored eyes. A very large entourage of frazzled-looking assistants hustled in behind her. Up close, she was even more beautiful than in the photographs Louise had seen of her, some of which were taped to the inside of her locker at school. She was tanner and more voluptuous than the pale, size 00 stars she saw in *Us Weekly* and probably only a few inches taller than Louise was. She was more real. But there was something luminous about her, too, as if she almost radiated. Louise noticed that Elizabeth had a faint white scar across her neck, probably from that recent operation she'd just read about. Louise decided she would have to watch the movie again once she got home now that she had actually seen all the actors in real life. If this could be considered real life. It was definitely a dream come true for Louise.

"This tunic is fabulous, but it's a little tight in the tummy. I had an extra steak last night, and this doesn't fit me like it did yesterday. Can you let it out a bit, Ireney? Pour me a little more champagne, love. This shoot is interminable. Although I don't mind when I'm shooting a scene with Richard. What do you think of him, Irene? Isn't he a dream?"

"Elizabeth, darling, don't worry, we will take care of

everything. Please have a seat. *Joan?* Where is my assistant?!" she heard Irene yell exasperatedly from the other end of the tent. "I need that belt immediately! As you can see, Ms. Taylor is here for her fitting."

"Sorry, Miss Sharaff." Louise frantically took one last look around and spotted a gold tasseled belt carelessly draped over a rack of white togas at the far side of the space. "Found it— I'm coming!" Louise shouted, palming the necklace and quietly shutting the lid of the rusted old trunk. She would just take a little souvenir home to Connecticut to prove that she was actually here on the set of *Cleopatra*. It was a memento like Irene said she kept from all her movies, Louise thought, justifying to herself what she was about to do. Besides, how else would anyone ever believe her? She decided to hide it under her blouse for safekeeping for the time being.

"Joan, we do have a movie to make here. Sometime this year, please! Sorry, Miss Taylor, I don't know what's gotten into her. She is usually so reliable."

"She's a little too elusive for an assistant, don't you think?" the actress replied, chuckling. "Why don't you borrow one of mine?"

Louise brought the supersize pearl necklace up to her neck, and no sooner had she clasped the delicate chain, then she collapsed to the sound of her film idol laughing her unmistakable deep, throaty chuckle. *At her.*

CHAPTER 13

When Louise awoke, she had a sinking feeling she wasn't in Hollywood anymore. She screamed. She was nose-to-nose with an intense-looking teenage girl who had tan olive skin, dark kohl eye makeup extending out past her brown almond-shaped eyes, a large hook nose, a thick neck, and a rather prominent chin.

"I didn't mean to startle you," the girl said tersely. She had a white ribbon tied around her head, and her dark waves were held back in a low bun with some escaped little pieces framing her face, much like Louise's own typical hairstyle. Her hair was a deep brown but with a reddish tint, as if she had used henna to color it.

"Oh, good, Charmian, you found it!" the girl continued. "Quickly, give it to me! I need to get back to my studies. An important Roman general is coming to the palace for dinner soon, and I have an idea I need your help with."

When the girl spoke, Louise caught a glimpse of her crooked yellowish teeth. Where she was now, they clearly didn't have orthodontists.

"Ummm...g-give what?" Louise stuttered, confused.

"Why, the pearl necklace I asked you to find, of course," the girl explained impatiently as she yanked a thin chain from around Louise's neck. *Ouch!* It was the same pearl necklace she had tried on from the trunk on the film set. Oh, why did she decide to take that necklace? She had finally found her dream job, was working for a famous costume designer alongside a Hollywood acting legend, and then she had to go and poke around in a trunk that specifically warned her against poking around. From experience, Louise knew she was going to need to keep an eye on that pearl necklace if she wanted any chance of making it home. But who was this girl? By the demanding tone of her voice, Louise had a feeling she had another boss to contend with. A boss who had just taken the iridescent pearl and gold chain—Louise's ticket home—and dropped it into her satchel before hurrying out of the room with a scarlet red silk cape trailing dramatically behind her.

Louise took a deep breath as she looked around the room to try to get her equilibrium back. She was never going to get used to this abrupt change of scenery. The warm air smelled exotic, like cardamom and spicy incense. She was in a grand bedroom with elaborate jewel-toned Persian carpets blanketing the white marble floors and a large raised bed that was twice as big as a California king mattress, with ivory silk sheets and a gauzy white fabric surrounding it. The lofted ceilings seemed about fifty feet high and made Louise feel like a dollhouse-size version of herself. Palm trees and spiky green plants were potted in large brown clay vessels around the room. She walked through an arched doorway out onto a blue-and-white-tiled balcony that overlooked a vast crowded city, and in the distance was a great sea filled with ships, their masts fitted with white billowing sails.

Louise looked down and saw she was now wearing a more primitive version of the gown she had tried on at the sale. It was a pleated dress dyed in a pale purple color, and it felt kind of scratchy against her skin, as if it was made of a rough linen fabric. It was much simpler and less luxurious than the lavender dress she'd tried on, but cut in a similar toga style, with two thick shoulder straps forming a deep V that kept the dress in place. The frayed, unfinished hem fell down to her ankles and just above her shoes—brown leather gladiator sandals that were at least two sizes too small and pinched her feet.

Meow. An elegant Siamese cat strolled regally into the bedroom, and Louise walked back inside and crouched down to pet it. The cat started purring and rubbing its head against Louise's legs as though starved for attention. Louise missed

her gray cat, Bogart, who was hit by a mail truck a few years ago. She was lost in a memory of him but was interrupted when a petite, dark-haired girl ran into the room, totally out of breath.

"Charmian, what are you doing?!" she asked, apparently horrified to see Louise petting the cat, which was now stretched out with its soft white belly exposed. "Don't touch that! It's a god!"

"Oops." Louise quickly shot up, startling the cat, which yelped and scurried out of the room. That cute house cat was considered a god? There was definitely a different set of rules here that Louise would have to learn if she had any hope of fitting in. The girl was wearing a marigold yellow variation of Louise's rustic dress, the color of which brought out the green in her eyes, and her black shoulder-length hair was braided with little gold tinkling beads securing the ends. She was very pretty, in an exotic sort of way.

"Cleopatra forgot her scroll of Homer's poetry," she said, holding out an enormous roll of paper. "You know how she hates to be unprepared and how much she loves *The Odyssey*. Do get it to her right away!"

Wait a second, that teenage girl I just met—the one with the enormous nose, frizzy hair, and bad teeth—is Cleopatra? But she didn't look anything like Elizabeth Taylor. In fact, there really was not any resemblance at all. Probably most people in the modern world, Louise included, thought of Cleopatra as being as beautiful as a movie star. But that girl wasn't even... pretty.

"Umm... Okay. But where did she go?"

"To the royal study, of course! She has lessons with her tutor, Pothinus, all day. Down the promenade and to the right," the flustered girl continued when she saw the puzzled look clouding Charmian's face.

"Is that—are you—Stella?" Louise asked hesitantly, hoping somehow that this girl was actually her friend and that they could be on an adventure together again. It would be so much more fun if she had someone to share it with.

"Stella? Who are you referring to?" asked the exasperated girl, who Louise immediately deduced was definitely not her fellow Fashionista. "I am Livia."

"Never mind," Louise replied, trying to mask her disappointment. "Of course, Livia, I will take it to her immediately." Louise clumsily took the carpet-size roll of papyrus tied with a red silk tassel and awkwardly rushed out of the room before she had time to ask Livia any more seemingly obvious questions.

CHAPTER 14

When Louise left the bedchamber and entered the covered arcade to deliver the mammoth scroll to Cleopatra, the first thing that hit her was the intense heat. It felt as if she were baking in an oven. It had to be over a hundred degrees! *Way* over, she thought, wiping a torrent of sweat already running down her face. She glanced down and discovered the back of her hand was covered with smudged red rouge and greasy black eyeliner. She didn't even want to know what Charmian's makeup was looking like right now.

The air wasn't like Connecticut in August, though. It was a dry heat, with no humidity, like being in a sauna...or a desert. *No humidity means no frizzies!* Louise thought, instinctively reaching up to her head and accidentally pulling off a bob-length wig. Wait, where was her hair? She dropped the scroll on the floor and frantically felt the top of her prickly head, which was shaved close to the scalp. Charmian was bald! Startled, Louise quickly put the dark braided wig back in place and nervously looked around to see if anyone had seen her gaffe. Luckily, no one had. She tried to check out her reflection in the polished marble wall and could barely make out a blurry version of her familiar face under a wig that was completely askew. She hastily adjusted her way-off-center part, picked up the scroll, and kept walking.

If she was with Cleopatra, then she was probably in Egypt, Louise deduced, halfway around the world and a few thousand years from her real life. *Whoa.* It was an exhilarating and terrifying realization. She had definitely never been this far from home before.

The scale of the palace was enormous, and Louise hobbled past an endless series of rooms connected by shaded open-air walkways, trying not to drop the cumbersome scroll along the way. She tottered down a magnificent hallway past a grand bubbling fountain with real brightly colored fish swimming in the blue-and-green-tiled basin, pausing to catch her breath and admire the intricate tile mosaics of lions on the floor, and the detailed hieroglyphic battle scenes carved into the limestone walls. She was a bit intimidated by the immense height of the towering Corinthian columns lining the walkway, but she laughed out loud as a monkey scurried past her and agilely climbed up a wide limestone pillar as though it were a tree. Exotic birds with electric blue and yellow feathers flew through the halls, singing and chirping as they darted from one lush green courtyard to another. It was like walking into the Egyptian wing of the Metropolitan Museum of Art, but, judging by the wildlife, it was real.

Following Livia's hurried instructions, Louise took a right at the end of the walkway and stepped through an arched cedar doorway into what looked like the royal library. She found Cleopatra, who Louise now guessed was roughly seventeen years old, sitting with her legs crossed on a low bench with a bright teal cushion in the middle of a school lesson. She had taken off her red cape and was wearing a matching scarlet-colored Greek-style flowing silk gown and intently listening while a tall, slender man read a passage aloud to her from a six-foot-long scroll. Strangely enough, the teacher was also wearing eye makeup and rouge and a long white robe. This must have been Pothinus. The scroll was so unwieldy it needed to be held by two male servants, who were wearing simple white sarongs and not much else. Apparently in this pre-iPad era, reading a book was a three-person job!

A diagram of a family tree of the different gods and goddesses was tacked onto the wall. The god Amun was noted at the top, and others with crocodile heads and mummy bodies continued below. Also hung on the wall were some extremely complicated-looking mathematical equations, the Greek alphabet, and Egyptian hieroglyphics. There were stacks of rolled-up

papyrus scrolls stored in cubbyholes on the far wall, and Louise couldn't help but compare it in her mind with her own classroom with its whiteboards and bookshelves. These scrolls were a lot different from the paper-bag-covered schoolbooks she was used to lugging around all day.

Once inside, Louise happily dropped *The Odyssey*, and it proceeded to unroll before her like a red carpet, dramatically announcing her arrival. Cleopatra shot Louise an intensely annoyed look, and Louise's palms were instantly clammy with sweat. *Oops*, another glamorous entrance!

Three handmaidens stood to one side, wearing a rainbow of brightly colored linen tunics and fanning the seated Cleopatra with large ostrich and peacock feathers. When Louise walked a little farther in, she was handed an oversize plume as well. The tutor stopped midsentence, and the two bare-chested servants hastily collected the scroll Louise had so gracefully delivered. Pothinus then began to read from that one instead.

Following the lead of the other handmaidens, Louise started to fan Cleopatra as best she could. It was a lot of work! After what felt like an hour but was probably only five minutes, Louise was sweating profusely and worrying that, with her luck, the green-and-purple peacock feather, which now felt as if it weighed as much as a brick, would slip out of her damp palms and land smack on Cleopatra's head.

Nevertheless, despite the manual labor, Louise couldn't help but ogle Cleopatra's outfit. She wore fabulous green-jeweled leather gladiator sandals, a much fancier version of the plain brown pair Louise was wearing, adorned with what must have been real sparkling emeralds! Even Christian Louboutin would have been jealous of those bedazzled shoes.

Louise could see by the entranced look on her face that Cleopatra was obsessed with Homer, and she wondered if he was like the J. K. Rowling of ancient times. Unlike what she had observed of Marie Antoinette, who struggled with reading and writing and didn't seem to take much interest at all in her studies, Louise could already tell that Cleopatra was incredibly smart and seriously into her schoolwork.

Pothinus paused and pointed at his only pupil, signaling that it was now Cleopatra's turn to recite part of the epic poem, which she did by heart. Her reading voice was beautiful, almost musical, and Louise found herself standing transfixed, mesmerized by the young queen's oratory skills. The handmaiden next to Louise shot her a searing look and nudged her to stop staring and keep fanning.

For the next part of her lesson, Cleopatra began practicing her hieroglyphics with a sharpened quill pen and black ink on a sheet of blank papyrus. It seemed much rougher and more fibrous than the loose-leaf paper Louise was used to taking her class notes or, more likely, doodling on. *How long did these lessons last?* Louise wondered, instinctively looking up on the wall for a clock that obviously wouldn't be there. They probably told time on sundials or some other ancient system. The school day was starting to feel as endlessly dull as it was at Fairview, and Cleopatra didn't even have other students or friends to distract her. Of course, Cleopatra seemed to be able to focus for a lot longer than the hyper kids in her classes. Louise had to admit she was excited to see that the legendary Queen of the Nile was actually kind of…a geek.

CHAPTER 15

"Excuse me, I must interrupt. King Ptolemy will be arriving shortly," a man wearing a long purple robe boomed at the entrance to the library, abruptly cutting off the lesson. Louise welcomed the interruption. Pothinus had roughly the same amount of inflection as Miss Morris, droning on about Alexander the Great and all of his military conquests, blah blah blah. She straightened up, smoothed out her dress, and hoped her wig was securely in place as her head was definitely sweating. Her wrist was starting to cramp up, too, from all that fanning, and she wanted to look somewhat presentable—she was about to meet the King of Egypt!

Louise was totally shocked, then, to see that King Ptolemy, who was carried into the room on a golden throne by four muscular servants in loincloths, was actually a chubby young boy, probably no more than ten years old. She bit her lip so she wouldn't giggle and completely give herself away as everyone stood as still and solemn as statues; no one else in the study was even smiling. It seemed a totally ridiculous and over-the-top way for a kid to travel from room to room. Couldn't he walk? The young boy was regally draped in a leopard-skin mantle clasped at the neck with a giant ruby brooch, and he wore a black braided wig under a golden crown that was too big for his small head. He was scowling and petting a sleek black cat curled up asleep in his lap. Apparently it was okay for a king to pet the four-legged deity, just not Louise.

"Hello, little brother. What brings you to this part of the palace?" Cleopatra asked sharply, obviously not happy to see him.

"I was so terribly bored. Let's do something fun," he answered in a high-pitched and already grating voice. The cat on his lap opened one eye and gave a wide yawn.

"You do know that I must study. And I strongly recommend you do the same," she said firmly.

He shrugged. "I don't feel like it. It's too hot to study." Ptolemy seemed whiny and irritating, like a typical little brother. Not that Louise knew much about that. She was an only child, but Brooke's younger brother, Julian, was constantly getting on their nerves and always bothering them whenever they hung out at the Pattersons' house, much to her friend's annoyance.

"Well, you can be ignorant if you like, but I must keep studying, as I haven't even started practicing my Latin yet,"

Cleopatra declared, shooing him out of the library with a dismissive wave of her hand.

"But you are always working. Why don't you want to play a game with me? Father is dead, so he can't make us study anymore."

"Exactly," Cleopatra replied. "Now we must take over his responsibilities. Have you even attempted to learn Egyptian yet? As Greeks, we must try especially hard to assimilate with our subjects."

The rulers of Egypt were...Greek? Weird, Louise thought. *We must not have gotten to that part in the movie yet.*

Ptolemy rolled his eyes at her as he motioned to his stone-faced handlers to get moving. "Suit yourself. Perhaps Arsinoe will be more fun," he said haughtily, and was immediately carried out of the room on his portable throne.

CHAPTER 16

Without any clocks, Louise could only guesstimate how long Cleopatra's school day actually was, but it felt like at least ten hours. She could hardly feel her hands from all the fanning, her left leg was starting to tingle with pins and needles, and she had to keep shifting her weight so her foot wouldn't fall completely asleep. It was a small miracle she didn't just topple right over. She had one precariously close call when the tip of her fan tickled the top of Cleopatra's forehead. The queen had swatted it away like an errant mosquito, but the girl next to Louise gave her a sharp poke in the ribs, and she quickly straightened up. They were allowed a few small breaks for water and fruit, but they never left the royal study all day. For each snack break, Livia would walk in with a platter of grapes or almonds and before leaving the room would pop one in her mouth. Louise looked on wide-eyed, convinced that Cleopatra would reprimand Livia for eating her food first, but she never did. It was the strangest thing.

When Cleopatra finally got up from her cushioned seat and put on her red silk cape, signaling the end of class, Louise let out an audible sigh of relief. She really hoped today was Friday, or however they told time in these days, otherwise this was going to be a really long week! And she thought sitting through Miss Morris's forty-minute history class was torture. At least she could sit!

As Cleopatra exited the room, the other handmaidens motioned that Charmian should follow her. Apparently Louise's new job was not to let the queen out of her sight. Louise trailed a few feet behind down the wide-open hallway, occasionally dodging a low-flying parakeet, unsure of what exactly she was supposed to be doing. A musician playing a wooden flute pranced along the walkway with the young queen, providing a musical accompaniment for her trip from school, like an old-fashioned iPod. Louise noticed that there were stern-looking guards with sheathed swords standing at attention at various doorways they passed.

"Charmian," Cleopatra called over her shoulder, "find my husband for me. I have an urgent matter that we must discuss."

Ugh, why did Charmian have to play such an active role? She wished she could just disappear into the background like the other servants, or walk around eating grapes all day like Livia. "Find who?" Louise asked, confused. She tried to think back to what she'd learned from the movie but could only remember the fabulous costumes. *Typical!*

"King Ptolemy, of course. Charmian, do you have heat-stroke?"

"The king? But I thought he was your brother?" Louise couldn't help but ask.

Cleopatra abruptly stopped walking, and Louise almost ran smack into her. She turned around, her face clouded. "That he is. In the name of Isis, I will not tolerate this insolence! Summon my brother to my chambers immediately."

"What? Never mind, of course, Your Highness," Louise replied, flustered. She hurried off in the opposite direction, her leather sandals nearly slipping on the slick marble tiles. *Is this normal for ancient times? Her younger brother is also...her husband? Could that be any grosser?*

And how was she supposed to find Ptolemy in this enormous and completely unfamiliar estate? She needed to get directions, stat. Louise stopped to ask one of the scary-looking guardsmen, who directed her to cross the courtyard, walk up a flight of stairs, through the throne room, down a spiral staircase, beyond the garden...and then her mind couldn't absorb another detail. Louise repeated it over and over in her head so she wouldn't forget. A GPS would have been a lot more helpful. According to her mother, thanks to her iPhone, she had never developed a sense of direction.

Finally she arrived at the door of the king's quarters, which were guarded by four extremely large and heavily armed watchmen. Ptolemy was meeting with his advisers. It looked strange to see a boy of ten and barely four feet tall giving orders to three grown men, one of whom was dressed in a full suit of body armor.

The moment Charmian was announced at the doorway, the men immediately stopped their conversation midsentence, leaving a chilling silence. "Speak. What do you want?" Ptolemy asked suspiciously. "Can you not see that we are in the middle of important royal business?"

"Your Majesty, Queen Cleopatra would like to see you in her chambers," Louise responded shyly. Ptolemy's squinty brown eyes narrowed into two angry slits. She awkwardly curtseyed as she had seen them do in some period movie, praying it was the right period, before excusing herself from the room as quickly as she could. She couldn't put her finger on exactly what it was, but something about the hushed meeting she had just interrupted gave her the creeps.

CHAPTER 17

Once she had gotten far enough away, Louise decided to take the scenic route back, mainly because she was completely lost. At least it gave her a good opportunity to explore her new home, which was beyond extravagant. Red-and-orange Oriental carpets lined the wide hallways, which were flanked with granite and marble statues of sphinxes. Many of the walls were decorated with pigment-painted scenes of gods and pharaohs standing stiffly in profile, occasionally depicting a human body but with an animal head, some carrying spears or musical instruments. Low couches draped in deep maroon-and-gold tapestry fabrics were sporadically placed throughout the palace and gave Louise a place to rest for a second and take in all of the amazing ancient artwork. She was starting to be overcome with that sleepy feeling she got whenever her parents stayed too long at a museum, as though taking in so much beauty was exhausting.

Interestingly enough, it seemed that as a handmaiden Louise could walk anywhere in the ginormous palace with never-ending wings and rooms and courtyards. It was as if she weren't even there—as if she were practically invisible. If Charmian were a spy, she would be in a good position to get the inside scoop. The halls were bustling with servants, armed guards, and toga-clad messengers who all seemed in a hurry to get somewhere and brushed by Louise without a backward glance. No one stopped her or asked her where she was going as she ran her hand over the cool limestone and marble walls while looking up at the tall, vaulted ceiling encrusted with jewels and gold, ebony, and tortoiseshell. It was beyond even the excesses of the palace of Versailles. There must have been hundreds of rooms all filled with ceramic pottery, plush ottomans and high-back armchairs upholstered in purple and red fabric, and exotic, spotted animal pelts covering the floors. Louise hoped Charmian wasn't responsible for cleaning all the guest rooms, too—that could take weeks!

Louise rounded a corner and ran smack into Livia. "What are you doing here? You should be preparing the master guest room before the Roman general arrives!" the delicate girl said, her green eyes nervously darting around as though someone were about to jump out from behind one of the Corinthian columns. Livia always seemed to be on edge for some reason, and her nervous energy was starting to freak Louise out. Livia led her into a large open bedroom suite, where she gave Louise a peacock-feather duster. Why was the girl always giving her work to do and yet seemed to do nothing herself? Livia leaned against the doorway and supervised Louise as she began dusting a teak side table covered with miniature mummy and falcon figurines.

"What do you do all day?" Louise finally asked. It seemed as if this girl just lounged around eating the queen's food and looked on while Louise and the other servants did all the work.

"Why, I am the royal taster," Livia replied in a serious tone.

"You mean you taste if the food is good?" Louise asked enviously. Next to being a designer's assistant, this girl pretty much had her dream assignment.

"In a way, I suppose I do," she replied, giving Louise a curious look.

"Can we switch jobs?" Louise asked. "I have a very refined palate," she added, thinking of all the new foods she was trying now that her father was cooking all her meals back home.

"I wish," Livia said wistfully. "But of course it is not our decision."

"Of course," Louise replied grumpily. She had lost a serious amount of decision-making ability on this particular journey, she thought as she swept the oversize feather duster across a massive vase filled with dozens of fragrant, fresh red roses.

"*Achoo!*" Louise sneezed, her nostrils full of ancient dust.

The vase would probably be in a museum under a locked glass case one day along with all the other little stone statuettes, but that didn't impress Louise quite so much now that she was the one required to clean them. Knickknacks, her mother called them. This palace was filled with them.

By the time Louise had finished her housework and Livia had led her back through the labyrinth of corridors to Cleopatra's wing, the queen was immersed in an intense discussion with her brother/husband, Ptolemy. Louise hovered outside the doorway so as not to interrupt, but she stayed close enough that she could still listen.

"The grain supply is being disrupted in the South, and because of this terrible drought, if we do not intervene, there will be a famine. We have to do something about this dire situation. You must defer to me. I know how to handle this crisis," Cleopatra said confidently. The assured tone of her voice made her sound much older than a typical teenager.

"It's not fair. You do everything," Ptolemy whined.

"That's hardly true. But I don't have time to argue with you. Let me mobilize the army and deal with this at once."

Ptolemy burst into tears of frustration. "It's not fair," he cried. Under the oversize gold crown and leopard robes, he was really just a little boy, no match for the intellect and poise of his sister. And judging by this tantrum, he knew it.

"You must support me and know that I will take care of it," she replied firmly. "There is a feeling of great unrest. And if the people sense that we are not working together, we will be overthrown. There are already small mobs starting to gather at the palace gates. Do not be foolish, brother."

"I am not foolish! You are!" He fled the room, pushing past Louise in a fit of rage. He hopped back up onto his portable throne, which was parked and waiting for him around the corner, and his dutiful servants swiftly carried away the sniffling child-king. Louise hesitantly walked in the doorway, not sure what sort of mood she would find her new boss in.

"Charmian, come in. Sit." She directed Louise to an ornately upholstered chair across from her at a wide table, which was covered in several large, curling maps marked THE NILE RIVER. "I feel as though I can trust you as you are my oldest servant." Cleopatra looked Louise directly in the eye for a long, uncomfortable moment, as though trying to gauge her loyalty. Louise had a moment where she wondered if Cleopatra meant *oldest* as in they went back a long time or if Charmian was perhaps really, really old. She brushed that tangent aside and nodded solemnly, trying not to let her gaze settle for too long on Cleopatra's wide, crooked nose.

"But I need you to swear on Amun that you will not speak a word of what I am about to tell you."

"Yes, my queen. You can trust me with anything." Louise had a feeling she was about to get some really juicy ancient gossip, although she did wish she had Stella there to share it with. What good was gossip if you had to keep it to yourself?

"And, of course, if I find out that you have so much as breathed a word of this to anyone, I will simply have you fed to the palace lions," Cleopatra stated plainly, as though throwing a person into the lion's den was a common practice during this time. Which perhaps it was.

Louise's mouth dropped open. *Yikes!*

Cleopatra must have registered the horrified look on Charmian's face as she grinned and said, "I am joking, of course." Louise relaxed. "I'd feed you to the crocodiles on the bank of the Nile River." This time she didn't crack a smile.

"Oh, my." Louise gulped. That was a pretty specific threat. Was this girl serious or was this considered ancient humor? Louise certainly didn't want to find out. She was definitely going to keep this secret as if her life depended on it, which it probably did.

"I think," Cleopatra paused dramatically, "that my little brother, my co-ruler, King Ptolemly, is planning to have me assassinated. My life is not safe here at this time. I fear that his tutor, Theodotus, and his adviser, the soldier Achillas, are guiding him in a dangerous direction. I have heard rumblings from my sources around the palace. Of course, I expected this, but not quite this soon."

Whoa! That ten-year-old crybaby kid was plotting a murder? Of his own sister? Of his own wife? Before Louise could wrap her twenty-first-century brain around what she had just been told, she swore she saw a shadowy figure dart away from outside the door. They were being spied on!

"Someone is out there!" Louise cried. She definitely did not want to take the blame if someone else spilled the beans. She had no intention of becoming lion—or crocodile—food.

"Who is there? Announce yourself!" Cleopatra declared. Silence. The hallway was now eerily quiet.

"I fear that I will end up in the same predicament as my dear sister Berenice," she continued a little more quietly. "As you know, she was killed by order of my beloved father and his supporters when she tried to usurp the throne. Beheaded." Cleopatra shuddered at the memory. "Her decapitated head served at dinner on a golden platter. I know that because of my power, I am also in a most vulnerable position."

These people are capable of murdering their own children, Louise thought in horror. She definitely did not want to be hanging around in this era for too long if even the royal family was not safe!

"Despite all the guards, I do not sleep well at night for fear of assassins. Ptolemy might have bribed my own men against me, for all I know. I can trust only you. From this night on, I need you to sleep with me here in my chambers for additional protection. This will be your pallet," she continued, pointing to a leopard-skin rug clearly made from a *real* leopard (the head was still attached!) lying at the foot of her bed on the other side of the vast room.

Louise nodded mutely. She was now totally freaked out, but in her current position, what choice did she have but to agree to this new perilous arrangement?

"We will speak more about this tomorrow. It is almost time for supper, and I must pray to Isis for strength and guidance."

Ohmigod, a murder plot? When Louise was Ptolemy's age, she was thinking about horses and her Barbie Dreamhouse. *Talk about sibling rivalry!* She guessed that Charmian was probably willing to take a bullet for her boss, but Louise herself wasn't feeling quite so generous yet. It was going to be a long night.

CHAPTER 18

That evening, before dinner, Louise was responsible for brushing and braiding Cleopatra's many wigs, while Livia once again sat off to the side and watched her work. Louise decided this was a good time to subtly get some information from her new acquaintance. "Did you know Berenice?" Louise asked her companion, who was reclining on a chaise, seemingly relaxed, but nervously picking at her cuticles.

"Yes, my sister had the honor of being buried with her in the royal tomb, forever serving her in the afterlife. Isn't that the ultimate honor?" Livia asked with almost a dreamy expression on her face. "I can only hope my life will do such service."

"I'm good," Louise replied quickly. "I'm not looking for any additional honors right now." Somehow being turned into a mummy alongside Cleopatra wasn't exactly the type of recognition she was looking for. She had final exams to take, a party to go to where she could see Peter again, which she was incredibly excited about. Considering she hadn't even had her first kiss yet, she wasn't exactly ready to get fossilized! "So people seem to get murdered all the time around here?" Louise asked hesitantly. Before Livia had a chance to respond, the girls were summoned by the other servants to join the young queen in the dining room for supper.

Louise stood at attention with her back against the cool limestone wall as she watched a girl about eight years old, dressed as a miniature version of Cleopatra in a long, pleated sea green sleeveless dress and seated at the table, fidgeting and waiting impatiently for the queen. She was draped in piles of sparkling jewelry and ropes of pearls, with big bauble rings on each finger, like a little kid who had raided her mother's jewel box and put everything on at once. She was a prettier version of Cleopatra, with the same olive skin and dark eyes, but with a more proportional-size nose and chin. Her mouth was set in a perpetual frown, though, which made her look as if she were sucking on a sour lemon.

Charmian was handed a heavy ceramic pitcher of water, which she assumed was to refill the goblets if they got low. Unfortunately, the cups were made of solid gold, so it was impossible from her vantage point to see how much water was in them. She prayed that the whole roasted pig displayed on the table wasn't too salty or they'd probably need a lot of refills! There were very few utensils on the table, only a couple of spoons, which seemed very strange to Louise. Did the royal family eat with their fingers? Platters of food continued to be brought into the dining room from the kitchen—and each dish seemed to get more peculiar than the last. An entire cooked antelope, which took four servants to carry in on a wide plank of wood, was followed by a plated gazelle, whose hooves stuck up into the air and slender horns were still attached, and an enormous ox, which was quartered and served alongside piles of onions and squash. These people ate animals Louise had seen only in dioramas at the American Museum of Natural History!

The thumping sound of beating drums and lyre music filled the air as a heavily made-up Cleopatra regally strode into the room looking statuesque in a long Grecian-style tangerine-colored dress made up of many layers of fine, sheer orange silks and a bright marigold sash. It was looser and more flowing than the skintight Egyptian sheath she was wearing earlier in the day. Louise now understood the difference Irene Sharaff had been talking about back in Hollywood. The intricately pleated fabric was tied on one shoulder and fastened with an emerald snake brooch, and, Louise noted, it looked like a lot of the dresses that have been going down the twenty-first-century red carpet lately. Thousands of years later and they are still making the same style fashion, Louise marveled. The queen had a sheer yellow mantle draped elegantly around her shoulders, long gold dangling chandelier earrings, and thick gold cuff bracelets with even more emeralds adorning both her wrists. This girl definitely did not do anything without a blinding amount of jewelry. Her thick black eyeliner was applied perfectly to show off her deep brown eyes, which were by far her best feature. With her hooked nose and pointy chin, she still wasn't conventionally beautiful in a fashion model type of way, but Cleopatra clearly knew how to accentuate her best assets. And her intense confidence almost dared you to say she wasn't the most gorgeous woman in the room. Louise imagined what it would be like to strut into the cafeteria with that attitude. And if not that, she could at least take a few makeup tips back with her to Connecticut to use once her mother allowed her to wear any.

As two servants materialized out of the background to pull out Cleopatra's heavy thronelike chair from the head of the table, Louise came to the conclusion that there were workers to cater to Cleopatra's every possible need: fix her hair, dress her, wash her, play music to accompany whatever activity she was doing, read poetry to her, carry her cup of water—everything, really. And everyone, except Louise, seemed to know exactly when and how to be of service. It seemed as if Charmian's job was to always be present in case Cleopatra needed anything, in this case a fresh glass of water, but not to say a word unless spoken to first. She turned to Livia, who

was standing next to her and seemed to be growing even more nervous by the second.

"Are you okay?" Louise whispered when she noticed the girl's hands were shaking. Livia shrugged and stared straight ahead, not saying a word, anxiously wiping her sweaty palms on the skirt of her tight yellow shift dress.

"Good evening, dear Arsinoe. Have you been waiting long, sister?" Cleopatra asked as she took her seat at the head of the table. They were the only people sitting at the long, overabundant table, being closely catered to by dozens of attendants.

The young scowling girl, who apparently was Cleopatra's younger and grumpier sister, greeted her sibling with an icy-cold stare. "Yes, in fact I have. Let us eat, shall we?"

A man in a floor-sweeping maroon robe brought out a jug of wine and poured a bit into Cleopatra's empty jeweled goblet. Louise was surprised to see Livia walk over to the table and pick up the queen's untouched glass and slowly bring it to her trembling red lips.

"I taste your food, daughter of Isis, and if there be harm, let the harm fall upon me." No wonder Livia was scared, Louise realized. She wasn't just checking if it was good—it was possible that whatever was served to the queen could be poisoned! A little anxiety was totally understandable considering her position could literally kill Livia. The royal taster's job was to try Cleopatra's food and drinks first, in case someone was trying to assassinate the queen. If something was poisoned, poor Livia would die instead. Louise guiltily acknowledged her relief that her coworker didn't take Louise up on her previous offer to switch positions—a little dusting never killed anyone. A toxic cocktail on the other hand...

The hesitant teenage girl took a tiny sip from the large goblet, and after a moment her striking green eyes grew wide as saucers. She stumbled, grabbing onto the arm of Cleopatra's chair before she convulsed and fell to the floor. Louise dropped her blue ceramic water pitcher onto the tile floor and watched helplessly as it shattered into a million fragmented pieces.

"Ohmigod, somebody help her!" Louise yelled, rushing over to her distressed friend. She shook the girl by the shoulders, as though Livia were just asleep, as though this were all just a bad dream.

The room was pin-drop silent as Livia twitched one last time and then lay completely still, her pretty eyes wide open, staring up at the arched ceiling. Louise had never seen a dead body before, but she just knew this girl who'd been standing next to her a second ago was gone forever. She had come close to death on her two previous adventures, but never had she experienced anything like this. Louise let out a scream.

Two linebacker-size guardsmen grabbed Louise by the arms and dragged her away from the lifeless body.

"Argh, Ptolemy! I'm not hungry anymore," Cleopatra declared briskly, standing up and throwing her solid gold spoon onto the mahogany table with a clatter. Immediately, the room started buzzing with servants removing from the table the poisoned wine and the untouched jewel-encrusted plates of roasted meats and vegetables. Other servants picked up the body of the recently deceased taster and quickly walked out of the room, carrying Livia over their head like a canoe. "Charmian, do be more careful with those water jugs. And I need a new taster," she called to Louise before she exited the dining hall. "Again!"

Louise lowered her head, hot tears streaming down her face. How could everyone be so callous? Someone had just died right in front of them and no one even stopped to notice!

Out of the corner of her eye, she couldn't help but notice a slight smile cross Arsinoe's lips, which to Louise seemed like a very strange reaction considering someone just dropped dead and her sister was almost murdered. She watched the young girl pluck an oyster from a display that had yet to be removed from the table and greedily slurp it down. Perhaps Ptolemy wasn't behind this particular incident after all.

CHAPTER 19

Louise lay down on the leopard-skin rug, trying not to look directly into the dead animal's preserved glowing yellow eyes. Cleopatra blew out the candelabra by her bed with one forceful breath. The room was thrown into near total blackness with just a sliver of moonlight streaming in through the gap in the curtained window. Louise was covered by a rough woolen blanket that barely reached her toes, and her head rested uncomfortably on a thin pillow that felt as if it were stuffed with a plank of wood. Even though the days were scorching, nights at the palace were very cold once the desert sun went down, and Louise shivered in only a coarse linen nightgown that scratched her skin and provided little warmth. After tossing and turning for a bit on the painful makeshift bed and replaying that evening's disturbing events, she resigned herself to the fact that she wasn't going to get any sleep.

"*Shhhh!*" Cleopatra scolded from behind the sheer silk

curtain that enclosed her luxurious platform mattress. "How am I supposed to sleep at all with you moving around so much?"

"Sorry," Louise whispered into the darkness. She silently started crying. She hadn't had the chance to get to know Livia all that well, but Louise couldn't help thinking about how young she had been, and now she was dead and no one seemed to care. There was a slight consolation in the idea that Livia truly believed she was doing her life's duty by serving her queen. She was willing to die for Cleopatra and felt that it would be the ultimate honor. But still…Louise held her breath and tried to will herself to keep totally still. The wool blanket was itching her left foot, and she quietly tried to rub it against the other without making any noise.

"Although, I cannot sleep anyway," Cleopatra said a minute later, a little more gently. "I miss her, too, you know. Livia and I grew up together. She and her sister were orphans whom my father took in to help keep Berenice and me entertained. I've known her since she was a little girl. But that is the way life is. I cannot have you being so sentimental, Charmian. We must be strong."

Louise sniffed. "I'm trying," she said, but secretly she was thinking, *I need to get out of here*. She didn't want to have to pretend to be strong anymore. She wanted to be herself. And, most of all, she didn't want to be next.

"I wish my father were still alive to guide me. Oh, Isis, please show me what to do."

Who was this Isis person Cleopatra kept praying to? Some kind of god? Like a cat? Louise knew she was going to have to do some research on ancient Egypt when she got home. *If* she got home.

"But I am glad that I have you here for my protection, Charmian. I feel like I can't trust anyone right now, not even my own family."

"Me, too," Louise whispered, although she didn't mean it anymore. If only she knew. How in the world was Louise, a twelve-year-old girl from the suburbs, going to protect Cleopatra, the most famous queen of all time, from anything? Particularly if her potential assassins lived under the same roof! What would happen to the history of the world if Cleopatra was murdered because Louise fell asleep and didn't warn her of danger? She had never had so much responsibility in her life. It was a miracle that her goldfish, Marlon, had survived as long as he did!

"I will protect you," Louise replied, much more bravely than she felt. But once she said it out loud, she felt more courageous inside. Maybe that was the way bravery worked.

"What if they have let out a poisonous asp in the palace, as they did to my favorite handmaiden, Alexas?" Cleopatra asked, alarmed.

A poisonous asp? Meaning, a deadly snake? Louise's eyes widened as she clutched the blanket up to her neck. "What happened to Alexas?" Louise couldn't help but ask, already knowing she probably didn't want to learn the answer to that one.

"It was so sad. The snake slithered under her bedsheets and attacked her when she was sleeping. Once the venom hit her bloodstream, she died almost immediately. She didn't even know what bit her, poor thing. But at least she didn't seem to suffer as Eiras did."

Louise gulped. She definitely didn't want to know what happened to Eiras, particularly if she ever wanted to sleep again.

"Tomorrow morning I will have my personal physician, Olympus, collect all the antidotes so they are ready in case we are targeted. We must be prepared for everything," the queen continued determinedly.

Louise felt the itch again on her foot and bolted upright on the floor, throwing off the bedding. *Ohmigod.* Was it the poisonous asp? She looked down, shaking out her wool blanket, but there was nothing under the covers, for now. A tiny mosquito buzzed around by her toes.

"Is everything fine, Charmian?" Cleopatra inquired, concerned.

"I think so," Louise replied hesitantly. "I'm not tired. I

think I'll just sit here for now and keep guard." Antidotes, deadly snakes, murder plots—what had she gotten herself into? If only she had never opened that trunk of source material. She couldn't help but feel as if this potentially deadly turn of events was some sort of punishment for stealing the pearl necklace from the wardrobe department. Louise was definitely feeling homesick for her own more mundane life in the suburbs. Bored as she was in class every day, boring didn't seem so bad right now. But if she was ever going to get back, she definitely needed to find that necklace.

CHAPTER 20

When she opened her sleep-crusted eyes and found the bright sunlight streaming in through the tall windows, Louise realized she must have miraculously fallen asleep after all. She turned over and screamed when she saw that she was eye-to-eye with a leopard, before remembering that the pelt of this deadly animal was actually her new bed.

"Charmian, why do you keep screaming?" she heard Cleopatra grumble from her much more comfortable setup a few feet away. "It's beginning to give me a dreadful headache."

"Sorry. Bad dream," Louise mumbled sheepishly.

"I need you to go down to the marketplace in Alexandria for me today. I would like for you to pick up some provisions for the dinner with the Roman general. I will need a sack of freshly ground cinnamon for the pastries, providing we make it to the dessert course, and some vegetables, but not the freshest ones, the ones that look almost rotten. And perhaps some old garlic and onions as well," she ordered from behind the sheer curtains, which Louise realized must also serve as protection from mosquitoes. Her own itchy legs were covered with bright red welts.

Rotten produce seemed like a rather peculiar request to serve at a dinner party for a famous general, but, of course, Louise agreed without questioning it. Her free will seemed severely restricted at this moment in time. And besides, she was excited to leave the palace (which was beginning to feel rather dangerous) and explore the city of Alexandria before returning to her ordinary life in Connecticut. She promised herself she would try to get back to the twenty-first century before things got even more perilous, but in the meantime, she was going to see the capital of ancient Egypt firsthand! And what better way than by shopping? Maybe she could even get some new sandals—Charmian seemed long overdue for another pair.

Cleopatra rang a tiny silver bell on her bedside table, and a line of handmaidens in matching gauzy white linen dresses entered the bedroom to get her ready for the day. "Send for Canidius. I'd like to hear some poetry as I bathe," she ordered. "Some lyre music would be nice as well."

One of the women handed Louise a new sheath, similar to the one she'd worn yesterday but dyed a drab muted beige color. The royals definitely got a much better wardrobe selection.

Louise was also handed a clay dish of something that must have been her breakfast, without any utensils. She suspiciously eyed the bowl of white mush—it was fish, and with the head still attached! Louise had never particularly liked seafood, and for breakfast it was even harder to stomach. She watched jealously as Cleopatra picked at a plate of juicy, ripe orange melon while wearing a comfortable-looking rose-colored silk robe and sitting leisurely on a mound of feather pillows. Louise felt her mouth water. She couldn't believe she was actually coveting a cantaloupe. Creeped out that her breakfast was looking back up at her and without taking a single bite, she discreetly set it down on a teak side table when no one was looking.

Following Cleopatra's instructions, one of the chambermaids gave Louise some empty burlap sacks for the vegetables and an embroidered silk change purse full of foreign money. Louise examined the variety of different-size silver and gold coins in her hand, wondering how much they were worth. Cleopatra noticed Louise studying the money and remarked over her shoulder, "Heed my words, one day my face will be on those coins. No other woman has ever had her profile on her own currency. I will be the first. One day I want my face to be recognized all over the known world."

"I can pretty much guarantee that will happen," Louise said with a bit of foresight. Little did Cleopatra know that she would become one of the most iconic figures of all time,

immortalized by everyone from William Shakespeare to Angelina Jolie. "The whole world will know your name for thousands of years to come," Louise assured her. Cleopatra looked pleased.

"That is exactly what I intend."

CHAPTER 21

Louise ran through the grand columned entranceway, down a wide flight of shallow marble steps, and bounded out of the tall, imposing palace gates, determined to start fresh and to explore as much of the old city of Alexandria as she could. Down the hill, she entered a wide white street guarded by two huge black marble sphinx sculptures that led into the heart of a crowded and lively walled city. The vast avenue seemed to be a mile across and was teeming with people shopping and selling their wares at tightly packed kiosks along the sides of the road.

Louise was immediately overcome by an intense array of smells that assaulted her nostrils. She could make out the rich fragrance of spices, the earthy scent of horses, cinnamon, incense, and the briny sea. Alexandria seemed to be a crowded and bustling port city. The merchants she passed were selling colorful silks, dried fruits, musky perfumes, and exotic oils, and

they all called out to her at once to come and try their specialties. She couldn't resist plunging her hand into a barrel of dried red beans and feeling the smooth small pods reach up to her elbow. The city was loud. Besides the cacophony of the venders, wooden carts clattered, rolling over the bumpy stone streets, and the competing melodies of various street musicians playing their lutes, lyres, and drums as they danced down the path fought to be heard.

Suddenly famished and remembering that she had left the palace without eating any breakfast, Louise bought a large purple fig from a young barefoot girl wearing a dyed pink piece of linen fabric draped over her left shoulder and tied at the waist. Louise strolled toward the sea, taking a juicy bite of sweet pulpy fruit as she watched the fishermen mend their nets. She paused to feel the salty sea breeze coming in from the Great Sea that made the air feel a lot cooler and more pleasant than up at the palace. In the midst of the choppy blue water, beyond the large wooden sailboats and intimidating military ships, Louise saw a light emanating from a towering lighthouse. It was like a skyscraper, at least forty stories tall! It was constructed of gray stone, with a statue of Poseidon, whom Louise knew to be the God of the Sea, and his giant trident perched at the very top. She suddenly realized she was looking at one of the Seven Wonders of the Ancient World. Not bad for a morning stroll!

She could have stood there all day, but unfortunately her feet were killing her. Her flimsy shoes felt as if they were made out of papyrus, and Louise was basically walking around on two pieces of paper. She should have worn Charmian's thin leather sandals. She hopped up onto the low stone seawall to continue her people watching and noticed that a lot of the men and women in the city weren't wearing any shoes at all. Most of the women were wearing simple pieces of dyed blue, green, or cream-colored linen wrapped around them and tucked at the waist. Many of the younger children had their heads shaved as Charmian did and weren't wearing any clothes at all! The men were dressed in kilts or loincloths. Apparently Marc Jacobs wasn't the first to try out this look— lots of men wore skirts in the ancient world! All of them— men, women, and children—were wearing kohl-rimmed eye makeup, and Louise wondered if it was less for fashion and more like how football players had black smudges under their eyes to somehow protect themselves from the strong glare of the sun. Considering Louise wasn't wearing sunglasses, the harsh late morning light should have been blinding, but surprisingly it wasn't.

Suddenly, Louise's ears caught a bit of a conversation going on a few feet away. "He was just a Roman puppet. Why will his heirs be any different?" said a man dressed in a soldier's uniform to his friend leaning against the wall.

"Hopefully the young Ptolemy does not worship the god Dionysus as his father did. The entire nation's coffers drunk away. Good riddance," he replied, spitting on the dirt in disgust. Louise realized they were speaking badly about Cleopatra's father, Ptolemy, who'd died recently! She discreetly scooted closer so she could hear their conversation better.

"And then the Greek had the gall to tax us. Not that he could tell us about it," the man laughed.

"No, he didn't speak a word of Egyptian! Too busy drinking wine to communicate with his people," the other said, shaking his head ruefully.

"And now the situation we're in. We are at the mercy of the Romans. I never thought I would see this in my day. Curse those Greeks!" The soldier extracted from his belt his long polished sword, which glittered in the sunlight.

"With this drought, it is doubtful there will be enough corn for the upcoming year. Meet me at the palace tomorrow evening. There will be a protest," the other whispered in a conspiratorial tone.

"I will inform the rest of the men," he said, placing his sword back in its sheath. *So the people of Alexandria are planning some sort of demonstration?* Louise hoped that it would be a peaceful gathering, but looking at the size of the sword attached to this man's leather belt, she had a sinking suspicion that wouldn't be the case. She needed to warn Cleopatra. It seemed the queen was right about needing to take action immediately.

Louise jumped off the wall to buy vegetables and head back to the palace before she was missed. But maybe she could squeeze in just a little more sightseeing, she thought, checking out an impressive-looking columned building that appeared to be some sort of temple. After all, how often was she going to be in Egypt? Particularly ancient Egypt! She skipped up a steep flight of marble steps and poked her head into the tall arched doorway to discover that it wasn't a church but rather the most impressive library Louise had ever seen! There must have been more than a hundred thousand scrolls, all tucked into their own cubbyholes, each one labeled with a gold tasseled tag. Intellectual-looking men with long black beards dressed in floor-sweeping white robes were pacing the room, intently discussing ideas and passionately arguing about philosophy, while others sat silently reading at dark wooden desks. Louise had a feeling that she'd be learning about these people in her textbooks in high school, or maybe even college. She overheard someone talking about how to measure the size of the earth using the projection of shadows. For a second, she wished she could slip them a piece of paper with $E=MC^2$ or another scientific discovery from the future that would totally blow their minds. She'd seem like an absolute genius. Before she had a chance to tamper with history, though, she was spotted.

"Excuse me!" yelled an old white-haired man, probably the royal librarian, as he carried an armful of scrolls past the entrance. "What business do you have in here?" he asked accusingly, dropping the rolled-up paper on a dark polished tabletop and heading surprisingly quickly in her direction.

"Oops, I seem to have lost my way!" Louise exclaimed as she ducked back out of the building, not wanting to cause a bigger scene. She wanted to draw as little attention to Charmian as possible and had to remind herself that she was in the body of a female servant and probably not even allowed in this library for two thousand more years.

CHAPTER 22

Louise filled her two empty burlap sacks with nearly rotten produce as requested, getting strange looks from the shopkeepers as she deliberately passed over the fresher vegetables. The sun was giving off its warm late afternoon amber glow, and she decided to head back to the palace before she had to find her way back in the dark. But after a few wrong turns, a frustrated Louise glumly admitted to herself that she was lost in a maze of alleyways that looked alarmingly similar. She turned another wrong corner and ran directly into a short, wrinkly old woman shrouded in a dark hooded cloak. "Let me tell your fortune, dear. It will only cost you eighty drachmas. Don't you want to know what the future has in store for you?"

"I'm pretty sure I already know," Louise responded, thinking wistfully back to her life in Fairview, a life that she was starting to miss very much.

"It won't take but a minute, dearie." The wrinkled old

woman, ignoring Louise's protests, grabbed her by the arm and pulled her onto a low, rickety stool by a small round table draped in a worn multicolored tapestry cloth. She roughly turned over Louise's right hand and began studying the lines on her palm. "Very unusual...I've never seen anything like this," she finally admitted, puzzled. "The tea leaves will help us decipher your path," she said, pouring a bit of tea from a silver pot and swirling the white ceramic cup filled with muddy-colored water three times counterclockwise. She turned the teacup over, dumping the hot liquid into a saucer, and eagerly looked inside. Louise glanced over at the bottom of the cup and saw nothing. It was completely clear and spotless, as if it had just gone through the dishwasher. "This has never happened before," the woman said, narrowing her dark eyes. "It's like you don't even exist."

"Thank you for your time," Louise interjected, trying to be polite and excuse herself before anything could really be discovered about her. She tried to get up from the table, but the woman yanked her back down onto the stool with a swift pull.

"Let me consult my crystal ball. You seem to be quite a unique case." This time the puzzled psychic pulled out a shiny, mirrored ball from beneath the table, and Louise realized that she was about to be in big trouble. From her two other time-traveling adventures on board the *Titanic* and at

the palace of Marie Antoinette, the one and only place where her true self could be seen by everyone was in the reflection of a mirror. She had quickly learned to avoid them at all costs. But before Louise could excuse herself again, the old woman peered down into her magic ball and saw Louise's real face, the face of a twelve-year-old girl from a different era, staring back at them, wide-mouthed, with braces and all. And, Louise noticed, annoyed, she seemed to have sprouted a bright red pimple on her chin. Louise, not Charmian, was reflected up at them, and she looked terrified. That was definitely Louise's cue to get out of there pronto.

"Who are you?" the woman asked harshly. "What are you?" She grabbed Louise's arm tightly so she couldn't run off. Louise was totally freaked out and having flashbacks to her terrible experience with Dr. Hastings on the *Titanic*, where she almost didn't escape.

"Ummm...it's a long story...I must go. Queen Cleopatra will be looking for me!" At the mention of Cleopatra's name, the soothsayer instinctively released Louise's wrist, but she continued yelling, alerting the neighbors, who were starting to gather on their balconies and trickle into the streets to see what all the commotion was about.

"You are not of this time! Are you an evil spirit?" the palm reader accused loudly.

Louise grabbed her overflowing bags of vegetables and

sprinted on Charmian's slippery paper shoes through the dark, narrow streets, fleeing the old woman before she was exposed for who she really was! She ran through a web of narrowing alleys until she eventually made it back to the main drag, just in time to see the sun dipping down in the horizon. Panting and utterly exhausted, she began to climb up the hill with her heavy burlap sacks filled of greenish onions and limp squash. It wasn't until Louise finally made it back to the palace that she realized she had forgotten the cinnamon.

CHAPTER 23

"Did you get everything I requested?" Cleopatra asked when Louise finally found her in a room that looked like a fancy Moroccan spa, soaking in a large tub beneath water spotted with pink rose petals. Louise had dropped the vegetables in the kitchen with the cooks and decided not to mention the missing cinnamon. There was no way she was going back into town after that harrowing experience.

"I left it all in the kitchen," Louise replied, not quite answering the question. The walls of the room were tiled with aqua green and turquoise blue mosaics of sea creatures, and in the center there was a massage table draped in blush-colored silk with glass bottles of different perfumes and oils all around. The steamy spa was lit with hundreds of white candles, and the scent of incense was making her head spin. There was a pretty pink-cheeked chambermaid massaging some kind of oil that smelled like coconuts into Cleopatra's dark, naturally curly hair, while another sat on the side of the tiled ledge playing a harp. Why couldn't she have come back as a queen instead of a lowly handmaiden, Louise thought grumpily. She longed to soak her painfully blistered feet and burning soles in the perfumed water.

"I've been thinking, Charmian, the Romans are so smug because they control the purse strings. My father was not wise to let our nation become so indebted to those barbarians. But I will show the general just how clever the Egyptians can be. And perhaps I will win back some of the land our father lost in the process," Cleopatra said determinedly.

"How?" Louise asked, excited to be privy to this political strategizing. She wanted to tell her about the conversation she had overheard in the city but thought it should wait until they were alone. Cleopatra never seemed to have much privacy, with all the servants and siblings and guests roaming around the palace.

"I have made a wager with him that I could host the most expensive dinner party he has ever attended. Charmian, I need you to bring me all the pearls from my jewel box. I have some experimenting to do. We'll see if my science lessons have paid off. I daresay they will prove to be very valuable."

Science? Dinner parties? Rotten vegetables? How is that going to solve anything? "Of course," Louise finally responded, having no idea what the strong-minded queen was talking about.

In any case, this request would be the perfect way for Louise to keep an eye on the pearl necklace that Cleopatra took from her the other day. She didn't think her aching feet and sore shoulders would be able to stand too much more indentured servitude in the ancient world.

"And do be careful, those pearls are worth more than all the gold in Egypt. You must guard them with your life." Louise was getting a little uncomfortable at just how often Charmian's life seemed to be put on the line.

"I will." She gulped. Whether she liked it or not.

Unfortunately, the pearl necklace was not in the jewel box with the others. Louise sat on a low magenta leather pouf in Cleopatra's massive walk-in closet. It was ten times as big as Louise's bedroom at home and filled top to bottom with headdresses and ceremonial robes and gowns. She frantically went through the contents of a grandiose ebony jewelry box for the umpteenth time. Piles of jewels of every color and every precious and semiprecious stone imaginable surrounded Louise. She had separated out a mound of pearls to give to the queen: pearl earrings, pearl rings, loose iridescent pearls, gray pearls, pink pearls, perfectly round pearls, irregular baroque pearls, but Louise figured Cleopatra must have kept that one particular necklace separate and hidden it somewhere else. But where? And why? She thought back to Arsinoe sitting at the dining table decked out in mounds of jewels and pearls—had she taken it? Louise stuck her head inside the dollhouse-size jewelry box one last time to no avail; the silk-lined chest was completely emptied of its luxurious contents. The necklace was most definitely missing. Before it fully sunk in that Louise was in perhaps the most serious trouble of her life, Cleopatra returned and announced the end of another day.

CHAPTER 24

"Olympus, have you been able to collect all the antidotes?" the queen asked the physician, a serious-looking bald man in a cream-colored toga. Cleopatra sat on a thronelike golden chair behind a wide ebony desk and wore a royal blue pleated sheath dress with a matching silk sash tied around the waist under a sheer green shawl. Today she had on a black braided wig ornamented with silver beads and a golden cobra.

"Almost all of them, Your Highness. I am still working on the venom of the Egyptian cobra."

"Do hurry," Cleopatra urged. "I fear what will happen if we are not thoroughly prepared."

Yes, please hurry, Louise echoed in her head. Without it, she worried, she would never get a wink of sleep. The previous night was another fitful one, when she managed to get only a brief rest as the sun started to rise. Her already overactive imagination was working overtime as a result of her current

sleeping arrangement. Every time she closed her eyes she saw Livia's trembling lips take a sip from the poisoned gold goblet. She always woke up screaming for her to stop, but it was too late. She was already dead. And if Louise didn't find the pearl necklace, she was afraid she soon would be, too.

Louise took a seat on a low marble bench off to the side and looked on, confused, as a bearded man with shifty blood-shot eyes was led into the sparsely furnished room. Olympus began tying him down to a long wooden table on a raised platform in the center of the room while Cleopatra dipped her pen into a well of ink as though she were in school getting ready to take notes. The red-eyed man looked exhausted and hardly struggled as his legs and arms were secured tightly with thick leather straps. As soon as he was restrained, a servant walked in carrying a large woven basket with a tightly fastened lid. He carefully opened the basket and, to Louise's horror, expertly pulled out a live, thrashing snake with his bare hands!

Cleopatra nodded her head, giving the snake wrangler the okay, and he released the brown-and-yellow-striped asp onto the table. It slithered and wrapped itself up the man's trembling bare leg. The snake let out a loud foreboding hiss, baring its sharp fangs, before it attacked and bit the man on the forearm, leaving two distinct red marks. The restrained man let out a pained yell as all the color drained from his face and his mouth fell open in a silent scream. Before Louise could even comprehend what had just happened, he convulsed, closed his eyes, and quietly took his last breath with a final shudder.

"He is dead," the doctor declared matter-of-factly after feeling the prisoner's pulse, or lack thereof, and dropping his limp arm.

Cleopatra nodded with a tight smile on her painted red lips. "That will do. Please take him away."

Louise sat there, mute and frozen, completely sickened at what she had just witnessed. She could not believe that this was her second dead body in only three days! Louise needed to get out of this dangerous era, and soon. People's lives were treated with no more importance than roaches. Louise saw all too clearly that she was expendable in Cleopatra's eyes. She could be immediately replaced. No one would miss her here. She needed to get back to a time where she mattered, where people saw her. She needed to go home.

How could Glenda and Marla allow her to travel back to such a perilous time? And then Louise realized with horror that they hadn't. They just sent her to a movie set, not some murderous ancient palace. She had chosen this experience by taking the necklace. And she was going to have to find her way back by herself, hopefully before another person croaked in front of her.

"A rather dignified death for a murderer, I must say," Cleopatra said, turning to her with a satisfied look. "That didn't look too painful, did it?" she asked Louise intently. "Next we will experiment with the toxic poison from the hemlock plant. So much crime these days, our prisons are overflowing. We are doing the city and the Egyptians a great service."

"What is this for?" Louise gasped, somehow finding her voice but still in a state of near total shock.

"Research," Cleopatra answered cryptically as she methodically recorded everything down in black ink on the papyrus scroll. From this angle, Louise couldn't read what Cleopatra was writing, but she had a feeling the title of this particular book was something like *The Most Deadly Poisons in the World* or *How to Commit the Perfect Murder*. The snake wrangler grabbed the bloodthirsty asp by the head and forced its wiggling and thrashing body back into the basket, securely retying the lid with a thick rope.

"Unlike the rest of my family, I want to be able to control my own fate," Cleopatra stated dramatically. Louise shakily stood up from the hard bench and left the room without excusing herself. She had seen enough for one day.

CHAPTER 25

Later that same day, when Louise had somewhat recovered from the morning's deadly events, she found herself in a rare moment alone with the queen in her chambers. "Your Highness, when I was in the market, I heard the people talking about the drought," Louise began and launched into telling Cleopatra about the conversation she overheard during her trip into the city of Alexandria. Louise was fed up with standing on the sidelines and holding her tongue. She wanted to help however she could and then get as much distance from ancient Egypt as possible, hopefully a few thousand miles and years away. "They are very worried that there will not be enough food—" Before she could mention the protest that was being organized, a panting messenger standing in the doorway interrupted her.

"My queen," he wheezed. "I need your signature as well as King Ptolemy's on these royal documents to decree the use of the Royal Army to intervene and protect the boats carrying the grain from the South to the ports of Alexandria," he gasped, seriously out of breath.

Cleopatra coolly grabbed the sheet of papyrus from his trembling hands and carefully read the paper before confidently signing her name. "Mine is enough."

"But—" the messenger began to protest.

"As I said," Cleopatra interjected, pausing dramatically while letting him squirm for a long, uncomfortable moment. "My signature is enough."

"As you wish, my queen," he conceded, seemingly terrified of Cleopatra. He quickly rolled up the signed sheet of papyrus and scurried out of the room.

Louise was impressed. Cleopatra was not afraid to show him who was in charge. She clearly had no intention of sharing power with her "co-ruler." Louise had a feeling it wasn't typical for a woman to sign her name on royal documents without her husband, although by now she had realized that Cleopatra was not your typical girl.

"Charmian, where were we? I need you to summon my sister Arsinoe immediately," Cleopatra commanded, turning toward Louise. "She has been so ill-tempered lately. I'd like to have a word with her," she continued, not giving Louise a chance to finish her story from the marketplace. Perhaps that decree Cleopatra just signed would be enough to help stop the famine and prevent any civil unrest.

"Since our father has died, I must act as both sister and parent to her. I can see she is already starting to resent my authority. Oh, Isis, please guide me."

I could use a little guidance, too, Louise thought as she sighed. For one, she had no idea where the pearl necklace was that got her into this situation in the first place. And on top of that, she was still completely lost trying to navigate her way around the palace. This estate was enormous, and the members of the royal family seemed to each have an entire wing to themselves. It could take her a week to find Arsinoe! If only she had never touched that pearl necklace. She could probably be at a Hollywood party right now with Elizabeth Taylor and Richard Burton, discussing the next day's costumes with Irene!

Louise knew better than to ask for directions from her boss. As Charmian, she should know all the answers already, and so she took off down the Persian-carpeted hallway as though she knew where she was going, praying that she had headed in the right direction. Louise paused when she heard King Ptolemy's distinct high-pitched voice from the other side of a tall door, which had been left carelessly ajar.

"We must get rid of Cleopatra! I want to be in charge all by myself, and she is ruining everything," he whined. Louise held her breath and cupped her ear to the wall so she could hear their conversation better.

"Of course, my lord," she heard a deep male voice respond.

"Leave it to us. We will make sure Cleopatra is out of the way for good and no longer able to bother you," another man said, followed by Ptolemy's hysterical laughter.

Cleopatra was right—her own brother wanted her dead! Louise peeked through the gap in the door and saw a group of grown men in dark robes gathered around Ptolemy in the midst of a heated discussion. The young king was wearing a regal purple cloak and sitting on a golden throne with his black cat curled up on his lap. Among these advisers Louise was surprised to recognize Pothinus, Cleopatra's tutor from the lesson the other morning. He was speaking with an older man draped in a long maroon cloak, who must have been Theodotus, and another one wearing soldier's armor, who Louise assumed had to be Achillas.

"And what about your sister Arsinoe?" Pothinus asked. "Shall we take care of her as well?"

"She is but a child," Ptolemy responded, which was ironic being that he was no more than ten years old himself. "She is no threat to me now. I will deal with her when the time comes." He once again burst into a fit of maniacal giggles, as though conspiring to murder his siblings was nothing but a funny game to him.

"All hail King Ptolemy!" the men said in unison as Louise backed away from the door before she could be discovered and accused of eavesdropping. She hurried down the hall. She needed to warn Cleopatra about this plot on her life before it was too late! She was the only member of this family who took the responsibility of leading Egypt seriously. The people needed her.

But first she needed to complete her duty and find Arsinoe. With the assistance of a few helpful palace guards, she finally found herself on the right path, arriving in front of a closed wooden door with a heavy bronze door knocker shaped like a lion's head, which she was told was Arsinoe's bedroom. Louise knocked once, but there was no response. The tall cedar door must have weighed a ton, and Louise had to push her whole body against it to get it to budge just enough for her to sneak inside. It was like trying to move a bulldozer.

She walked in to find the young girl playing with a group of miniature handmade wooden dolls dressed in little brightly colored scraps of silk and linen fabric. Arsinoe was wearing a dyed indigo linen sheath dress with gold-embroidered trim and jeweled shoulder straps. Gold bangles stacked up her small arms, but this time she wasn't wearing any necklaces, much to Louise's disappointment.

Her first impulse was to get down on the rug and start playing with the girl. She really needed a friend right about now,

and Arsinoe probably wasn't that much younger than Louise. *She seems so sweet*, Louise thought, thinking maybe she had misjudged her the other night. That is, until she noticed what the young girl was playing with her dolls. Arsinoe was staging a tiny war.

"Take that, Cleopatra!" the intensely focused child yelled, clobbering one of the figurines and practically decapitating her in the process. "My army will destroy yours. I will be the most powerful ruler of the land. You and Ptolemy will have to answer to me!" The little girl was so intent on her violent game that she didn't even realize Louise was standing in the room watching her from a few feet away.

Louise cleared her throat, and a startled Arsinoe dropped the dolls and gave Charmian an icy-cold stare. "What do you want? Can't you see that I'm busy?"

"Cleopatra would like to see you in her chambers," Louise replied.

"No one tells me what to do!" Arsinoe replied haughtily.

"She asked that I come fetch you at once," Louise said more firmly, using the tone of voice she reserved for when the neighborhood kids she was babysitting wouldn't go to bed.

"I hate Cleopatra," Arsinoe said in a sinister voice that led Louise to believe that she really meant it.

"But she's your sister," Louise replied, shocked at how angry Arsinoe was for such a little kid.

"So what?" The young girl gritted her teeth and stepped on the head of the doll with her leather slipper, splintering the toy into two jagged pieces. She nearly pushed Louise over as she stormed out of the room. Siblings like these made Louise happy to be an only child!

CHAPTER 26

It was the night of the dinner party with the famous Roman general, and all of the palace staff was rushing around to make sure that every gold-plated fixture and mother-of-pearl-studded doorknob was shining. After her stern talk with Arsinoe, Cleopatra had spent the remainder of the afternoon getting groomed and bathed with various sweet-smelling oils. Louise was once again relegated to brushing and braiding her many wigs. The chore seemed totally excessive considering the queen could wear only one at a time anyway. Meanwhile, another group of servants prepared several ceremonial dresses for the discerning ruler to choose from. These dresses were made of fine, beautifully dyed silk and were much tighter and more formfitting than the flowing pleated Greek- or Roman-style gowns. It would take several handmaidens to squeeze Cleopatra into whichever one she selected. They all had wide shoulder straps embellished with precious stones and shimmery gold embroidery holding them up.

Shortly before the general was due to arrive at the palace, Charmian was taken off wig duty and dispatched to the dining room with some of the other girls.

The hallways were lit with flaming torches, which cast dancing shadows around the marble palace walls. There were platters overflowing with an abundance of fresh figs, dates, pomegranates, and almonds on every polished tabletop along the way, and Louise swiped a bunch of ripe purple grapes from one of the bountiful fruit baskets as she passed. She was starving. It seemed as though the only meal Charmian was ever offered was plate after plate of bony fish. Louise said a little prayer that these particular grapes weren't poisoned before hungrily popping the juicy fruit into her mouth. Being by the sea and the Nile River seemed to limit the food options for the servants, at least. The royal family, on the other hand, had access to almost anything imaginable. Walking through this luxurious setup, it seemed impossible that there would soon to be a famine to contend with or that the country was deeply indebted to Rome.

When they arrived at the dining hall, glowing magically with the light of hundreds of white candles in candelabras, Louise was once again handed a pitcher of water. The vessel was made of solid gold and extremely heavy. Louise sighed. It was probably going to be another long night. Still, she guessed she should consider herself lucky that she had not been promoted to Livia's position as royal taster for this meal. Her job might be boring and uncomfortable, but at least it wasn't going to kill her...yet.

Louise took her place against the wall with the other servants as the apparently famous Roman general (although Louise had no idea who he was) entered the dining room proceeded by several guards in brick red togas. He was deeply tan, muscular like an athlete, with thick brown wavy hair. Actually, he was pretty cute, Louise admitted to herself. He wore polished bronze armor with a falcon embossed on the breastplate under a heavy burgundy cape draped across his broad shoulders. His brown leather boots were laced up to his knees, beneath a pleated kilt. The general was directed to sit at one end of the long banquet table, which had been covered in colorful silk tablecloths. Cleopatra's throne stood at the other.

The thumping rhythm of beating drums resonated throughout the hall, and the tall, heavy wooden doors were flung open as Cleopatra made her grand entrance into the dining room, followed by a troop of scantily clad dancers, gymnasts, and fire throwers. Louise had never seen the queen look so powerful and luminous. She had decided on a long, sleeveless silver shift dress in the traditional Egyptian style, accented with metallic threads and intricate beadwork. The outfit was so tight around her legs that she had to walk with small, deliberate steps. It was like the first bandage dress, Louise thought, and Hervé Léger may have owed a small debt to the queen. And as if the gorgeous gown wasn't enough, an elaborate headdress with three golden snakes intertwined at the crown adorned Cleopatra's head. Pearls had been woven into her dark wig and looked like little flecks of light. Louise smiled at the effect proudly. She had done a pretty good job on that one. A gold snake bracelet wrapped its way around the queen's thick upper arm, two gigantic pearl teardrop earrings hung from her ears, and, Louise suddenly noticed with a huge wave of relief, she was wearing the missing pearl necklace Louise had been so frantically looking for!

"She has bet the general that she could host the most expensive dinner party in the world," whispered the handmaiden next to Louise, who was holding a single golden spoon. Veiled performers twirled around the banquet hall in colorful figure eights.

"I know. I bought the vegetables, but there's not even any food on the table," Louise said, confused, looking down at the empty gold plates. *And why does* she *get the job of spoon holder?* she thought grumpily, adjusting the heavy pitcher in her sweaty hands so she wouldn't drop it again.

"Just wait," the girl responded. "Quiet, the dinner is about to begin."

"I see you are one for clever games. What shall we wager?" the Roman asked confidently once the music subsided and the

acrobats with their flaming torches had all pirouetted out of the hall.

"Whatever you please," Cleopatra said sweetly. "But let us make it worth your while. The Eastern Provinces perhaps?"

He chuckled. "As you wish. Bring on the first course. You know I can never refuse a beautiful woman," he said flirtatiously. "Particularly one who claims she can consume the wealth of an entire nation in one supper." Even though Cleopatra wasn't typically beautiful, she definitely was confident and seemed to have a charmed effect on powerful men, or at least this particular one.

The kitchen staff paraded into the room in an organized procession and brought forth a rather unimpressive, small whole roast fish with its beady eyeballs still attached. A few plates of sad-looking wilted squash and onions from Louise's purchases were the side dishes, and Louise watched as everything was placed on the table in front of the general. The Roman guest looked on smiling, as though he had already won. "Is this the best Egypt has to offer? You must come to Rome, and we can show you what a feast really is."

"Oh, I am sure you have extravagant dinners in Rome, but unfortunately I am rather busy right now dealing with a grain situation, and traveling does not seem possible at present."

"Perhaps another time, then," he replied with a wink.

"Perhaps." Cleopatra did not seem impressed. "But if this

is not up to your Roman standards, we do have one additional course." Cleopatra nodded to a servant wearing a purple sarong and standing at attention. The servant walked over with two large golden goblets and placed one in front of the queen and one directly in front of the general. The handmaiden next to Louise walked over to the table as well and took her place behind the queen. Louise hoped, for the girl's sake, that she wasn't the one to have inherited Livia's old job.

The confused guest sniffed the contents of the goblet disdainfully. "Vinegar? Surely the wealthiest woman in the world can do better than that."

"Oh, surely she can." Cleopatra smiled knowingly and reached up to her neck as if to unclasp her necklace. Louise gulped nervously. That pearl was her only chance of getting out of here. What was Cleopatra planning on doing with it? The queen paused for a moment, as though she were a chess player considering her next move, and then took off her left earring instead, a creamy pearl so large the weight of it stretched out her elongated earlobe. It seemed as though the entire room took in a collective breath, tense with anticipation. Without hesitating, Cleopatra dropped the earring into the golden goblet of vinegar. The drink began to hiss and spit as though she had thrown an Alka-Seltzer tablet into a glass of water as Louise's grandpa used to do.

The Roman looked on in wide-eyed shock as Cleopatra

stirred the bubbly liquid around with the long, golden teaspoon handed to her by the handmaiden Louise was talking with before. Cleopatra nonchalantly picked up the cup, as though she were merely stirring sugar into her tea. "We did say the Eastern Provinces, did we not?" she asked, smiling at her now clearly uncomfortable dinner companion.

His previously flirtatious eyes turned cloudy with anger as the realization that he had been outsmarted quickly dawned on him. Cleopatra had just made the most expensive cocktail ever. When the bubbling finally subsided, she raised the cup to her ochre-stained lips and took a delicate sip.

"A bit rich for my palate," Cleopatra said with a sigh. "You do know how much these pearls are worth, do you not? For the other I could probably buy the Parthenon or a small nation." He nodded mutely. She gulped down the rest of the drink while looking him directly in the eye, savoring her victory. "Now, shall we eat?"

Another army of waiters marched into the dining room from the arched doorway, this time carrying impressive platters of crackling boar, a towering arrangement of oysters, and a whole cooked flamingo!

"I'm not hungry anymore," the Roman general declared, abruptly standing and nearly knocking his heavy claw-foot chair over as he furiously stormed out of the room with his befuddled security detail trailing behind him.

Cleopatra turned toward Louise. "Oh, well," she muttered. "I suppose this will be a short visit. But wasn't that great fun, Charmian?"

Louise smiled and nodded, totally impressed by the queen's boldness and, most important, relieved to see the necklace still securely clasped around Cleopatra's neck, the pearl not dissolved. She still had a chance of making it home, and she couldn't wait to tell her mom that vinegar, Mrs. Lambert's favorite condiment to drench all of their food in, actually did have some magical properties after all!

CHAPTER 27

"Wake up," a husky voice whispered urgently into the darkness.

Louise had finally fallen asleep after a long stare-off with the taxidermic leopard she was lying on. She had felt much more relaxed knowing that the magic necklace was still within her reach.

A woman in a hooded wool cloak abruptly shook her awake. "What's going on?" Louise asked, alarmed and still half asleep in a groggy dream world. *Were they in danger?* She rubbed her eyes and through the darkness realized that it was actually Cleopatra standing over her and looking rather ordinary without any makeup or jewels on.

"Let's go into the town in disguise. They will never know it is me," she said, looking more like a mischievous teenager than a serious queen. Louise supposed in a way she was both.

"Awesome!" Louise exclaimed, feeling for the first time

as if they could almost be friends and take a break from this queen-servant dynamic they had going on. She jumped off her pelt and wrapped herself in the itchy beige cloak that Cleopatra held out for her.

"Awesome?" Cleopatra repeated, confused. Louise had to remember to take that word out of her vocabulary for good.

"You must not forget your wig," Cleopatra chastised, handing her Charmian's braided hairpiece. Louise had actually kind of gotten used to her new closely cropped haircut. It was pretty liberating to not have to worry about how to flatten down and tame her natural frizz every second of the day.

"I thought we could go down to the kitchen," the queen said conspiratorially, "and gather some eggs to bring with us..."

Wow, we're going to egg people's houses? It was like mischief night in the suburbs. Her mother would kill her if she found out what she was up to. For so many reasons!

"...and then we can leave them by the townspeople's doorsteps, so when they wake up they will find the eggs and it will be like a gift from the gods, an offering from Isis during this difficult time."

Louise smiled, feeling a tad guilty that she thought they would throw the eggs, not leave breakfast. "That sounds like a great idea. Let's go!" But before they had even left the room, they were interrupted by a commotion at the bedroom door. A sweaty messenger wearing a linen loincloth and worn leather sandals was ushered in by two burly watchmen.

"Your Highness, I am sorry to interrupt you so late in the evening, but I have just received word that Arsinoe and her tutor have fled the palace," the flustered boy said. "She is angling to be declared queen by the people," he continued, averting his eyes. At that news, the guards escorting the messenger grabbed his arms so he couldn't escape.

Cleopatra froze, clearly shocked by this surprising turn of events, and a nervous electricity suddenly filled the air. Louise was reminded of that saying "don't shoot the messenger" and wondered if it originated during ancient times. "Ambitious little child," Cleopatra finally replied with a slightly admiring smile on her lips. "But that will not do." Her brown eyes had turned cold and dangerous, as if Louise were looking at a totally different person from the giddy teenage girl who just a few minutes ago wanted to sneak into the town wearing a disguise. "Do you have other news?" she asked the now visibly trembling boy, who shook his head no. "Then you are dismissed," she ordered as the guardsmen let go of his arms and the terrified messenger darted out the doorway. "Everyone may go!" she yelled, and the three-hundred-pound Mack truck-size men slunk out behind him like scolded schoolchildren.

Cleopatra began furiously pacing the room, thinking out

loud and calculating her next move. "Isis, please show me the path. Do I warn Ptolemy?"

Louise realized that now was her chance to warn Cleopatra about what she had overheard. After seeing the icy-cold reception the last messenger with bad news had received, Louise was a little hesitant to put herself in that situation, but she knew she didn't have a choice. She didn't know if she had the power to change history, but she had to at least give it a try.

"Your Highness," Louise began, clearing her throat. Cleopatra stopped pacing and turned toward Louise as though she had forgotten she was even in the room. "Your Highness," Louise repeated with a little more confidence. "Do not trust Ptolemy. You were right about him. It's not safe here for you. I overheard him talking with his advisers. Even your tutor Pothinus is in on it," Louise rushed, trying to get everything out. "He doesn't want to share anything. He will never be happy to just be co-ruler."

"How will he lead?" she scoffed. "Ptolemy is a selfish child. He is no ruler. He cannot even speak to the people directly as he has not bothered to learn their language. But Arsinoe?"

"Well, from the way that she plays with her toys, I am pretty sure she'd like to be finished with both of you," Louise confided.

"She is but a child."

"I know, but you have to be careful. I swear you were right

about them. You are the only one who can lead your people," Louise pleaded.

"When did you learn of this?" Cleopatra asked suspiciously. "Why have you not informed me of this earlier? I can have you killed for conspiracy, you know. I thought I could trust you, Charmian."

Louise gulped. This was not exactly turning out as she had planned. Just then, the angry queen put her finger to her lips and cocked her head like a jungle cat listening for a predator in the distance.

"Did you hear that?" Cleopatra whispered, rushing to the balcony door.

"Hear what?" Louise asked, and then she did. It was a low rumble coming from outside. It was a sound Louise was now all too familiar with, like the sound of a thousand hungry French peasants storming Versailles. It was the sound of an angry mob.

Louise followed Cleopatra to the balcony, and they peeked through the long white curtains to discover that a swarm of people had begun to gather outside the palace gates. They were holding torches and bricks, and they were shouting and shaking the tall gold bars that surrounded the royal estate. News of Arsinoe's escape must have gotten out. The uprising had begun. Perhaps Louise was too late in delivering the news after all.

Surveying the situation, Cleopatra snapped to attention like a general. "Charmian, prepare my trunks at once. We must leave immediately through the rear gates. There is no time to spare. We will go under the cover of darkness to Syria, where I can gain the support of the Egyptian people. They *will* follow me, I have no doubt. Once I gain their loyalty, I will come back and reclaim my throne. You must help me pack. *I will not be triumphed over!*"

Louise nodded in awe of how quickly and confidently the queen was able to make such important choices. She spent more time just figuring out what outfit to wear to school in the morning! Louise had some decisions of her own that needed to be made. The sound of the mob outside was a low constant thrum; and she knew that if she went with Cleopatra to Syria, there was a good chance she would never come back to Egypt, let alone her real life. The glow of flames from the torches outside cast angry shadows around the room.

She knew that it was definitely time to find the necklace and head back to Connecticut. Or Hollywood. Or anywhere, really. Anywhere had to be safer than ancient Alexandria on the eve of a revolt.

CHAPTER 28

Louise rushed into Cleopatra's closet to begin organizing her trunks and to try to retrieve the pearl necklace to make her own eleventh-hour escape. She shouldn't have been shocked to discover Marla and Glenda had finally decided to pop up, but she was, and a startled Louise let out a slight squeal of surprise upon seeing them dressed for the times and raiding Cleopatra's personal wardrobe.

Marla was stuffed into a tight yellow Egyptian sheath dress like an Italian sausage, her thick ankles tautly laced into matching lemon yellow gladiator sandals. The dress was so tight, Louise could see her outie belly button protruding from her midsection like a turkey thermometer.

"Why do I always end up in these form-fitting numbers, Glenda? To painfully remind me that I've gained a few pounds over the years?" she asked her cohort with a grimace.

Glenda, wearing a flowing Roman-style kelly green toga

dress that complemented her flaming red hair, was devouring a pile of figs dripping with honey off a gold platter. "Now, we've never been here before, but what a fabulous adventure! Have you tried these figs? Heaven-sent!" she exclaimed, the stack of gold and silver bangles on her arm clattering with every bite. Both women were wearing red matte lipstick and heavy eye makeup, thick black liner and cobalt blue shadow, extending up to their penciled-in eyebrows, which made them look like Egyptian cartoon characters.

"Oh, I suppose one won't hurt." Marla helped herself to a plump fig, and Louise swore she heard the sound of the seams on her dress ripping one by one with each bite.

"Jesus," Louise muttered under her breath. "How can you eat at a time like this? Please help me out here!"

"Nope, Jesus hasn't been born yet. Try not to give yourself away, my dear," Marla tsked.

"Yes, they are very quick to murder in these times. No reasons needed. This was a bloodthirsty society, as you may have noticed by all the people dropping dead around here. And that ghastly science experiment with the poisonous snake... We would never have sent you to such a dangerous time. You do know how to get yourself into a jam, my dear."

"Ooh, fig jam would be mahvelous!" Glenda exclaimed, polishing off the last of the overripe fruit and tossing the empty platter onto a nearby divan.

"And I am quite sure that *stealing* jewelry is a punishable offense as well," Marla remarked, throwing Louise a pointed look. "What do they say? An eye for an eye? A pearl for a... Well, I can't quite remember how that part went." Marla was now trying on Cleopatra's various headdresses and currently had a gold vulture attached to the top of her head. "Not quite my style," she decided, taking off the ornate bird.

"I'm sorry," Louise said. "I know that it was wrong to take that necklace. Believe me, I'll never do *that* again."

"That Roman general is quite handsome, isn't he? Talk about famous. Forget about *Us Weekly*—think about Shakespeare! Oh, yes, this is certainly an adventure. Perhaps we should thank you for your little indiscretion," Glenda responded, ignoring Louise's attempt at an apology as she dabbed a bit of Cleopatra's almond oil behind both ears.

"I think I'm ready for this adventure to be over," Louise said. "I'm ready to go back home now."

"Well, I suppose we'll find out what happens when you stick your nose into a trunk that says KEEP OUT. But I must admit this has been quite fun for us! New inventory! Who knew they were so fashionable over two thousand years ago? I had no idea that by ancient standards, Alexandria was like Paris, or Milan!" Glenda exclaimed, wrapping herself up in a long square of sheer magenta fabric.

"Vintage might not be the word for it, but Cleopatra was

quite stylish for such an antiquated era," Marla continued, this time trying an elaborate topaz-studded headpiece on for size. "Absolutely fabulous! Have you seen the size of these emeralds?" she asked, greedily grabbing a sparkling green collar necklace off the table.

"And they're all real! And the pearls? To die for. Oops, I suppose you do know about those. You'd think you wouldn't be able to lose something that *big*," Glenda admonished, clicking her tongue with disapproval. "It would take a life of indentured servitude to pay for that necklace. In fact, if you don't find it, that may be just what's in store for you! Do you mind pouring me a glass of water?" Glenda asked with a mischievous sparkle in her eyes. "These desert conditions do make one quite thirsty."

"I'm off duty," Louise grumbled. "I'll find the necklace. It's got to be around here somewhere. I wouldn't mind some help looking, though. My mother is probably really worried about me," Louise said, missing her mother very much. She wondered if she would ever be able to talk to her about these adventures. Maybe she would have some advice as how to get out of the predicaments she always wound up in.

"She probably is, poor dear. Although she wasn't always such a nervous Nellie," Marla responded, shaking her head sadly, which was now adorned with a jade-encrusted cobra.

Louise was about to ask again how Marla had such insight into her mother's state of mind, but Glenda interrupted.

"Well, best of luck, dear! You do know this palace is one-third the size of Alexandria? But I'm sure you'll find what you're looking for. Where did you uncover your last treasure?" she asked cryptically while wrapping herself in another layer of eggplant-colored silk and looking more and more like a colorful mummy.

Louise heard Cleopatra call from outside the dressing room. "Charmian, have you prepared my trunks?" she asked urgently. "We must depart immediately."

"I'm working on it," Louise replied quickly. "I just need a few more moments." Before Louise turned back around, the spicy smell of incense and sudden burst of violet-colored smoke alerted her that the witchy salesladies had disappeared as quickly as they'd arrived. Once again, Marla and Glenda were not going to help her out of the mess she had somehow gotten herself into. They showed up only long enough to remind her that she needed to help herself.

Louise walked over to a barred window and peeked down at the crowd through the ivory linen curtains. The sound of the angry mob outside the palace gates was now deafening. Louise felt like she was back in the French Revolution. In the olden days when people were upset, they certainly let you hear it. Men were now trying to scale the tall gates, others were launching flaming torches, and some were demanding to see King Ptolemy.

"The caravan has been organized. Collect my jewelry box, and I will meet you by the back staircase in a few moments," Cleopatra told her.

"I'll be right with you!" Louise cried, trying to keep it together. She knew she had only a couple of minutes to find the necklace and make her escape.

Louise opened Cleopatra's enormous jewelry box on the low wooden table and once again searched desperately for the pearl necklace. She pulled out gold cuff bracelets, long dangly jade earrings, rings with humongous amethysts and rubies, and what seemed like a ton of gorgeous and insanely expensive jewels, but where was that one invaluable necklace?! Cleopatra was definitely wearing it at the dinner with the Roman general, so it had to be around here somewhere. *Where did she find her last treasure?* She remembered back to the trunk in her closet, where she uncovered her mother's photo and realized it could be hidden in a secret compartment or false bottom. She ran her fingers along the bottom of the silk case, and eased the edge of the fabric off. Underneath she felt the delicate chain and triumphantly yanked it out of the box.

"The queen is ready to depart," she heard a deep male voice announce from the other room. It was time for Louise to leave Egypt as well.

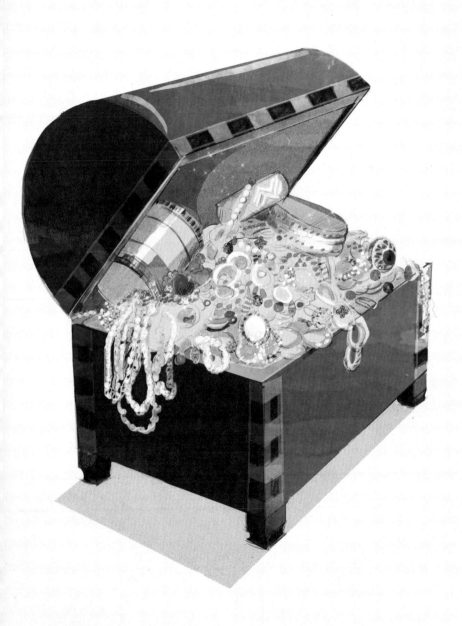

"Almost ready!" Louise yelled, hoping to buy herself another second so she could make her escape.

She clumsily attempted to secure the thin gold chain around her neck and was fumbling with the delicate and complicated clasp just as one of Cleopatra's burliest and meanest-looking bodyguards walked into the dressing room and saw Charmian surrounded by the queen's priceless jewels while trying to smuggle out perhaps her most valuable necklace. *Oh, no*, Louise realized. She could definitely see how this might be misinterpreted.

"It's not what you th-think...." she stuttered.

"Thief!" he yelled, alerting the security in the other room as he rushed toward her and reached for his sword that hung in a case on his leather-studded belt. "In the name of Isis, put that necklace down."

Her hands shaking and without a moment to lose, Louise managed to hook the solid-gold chain in place. In that instant, she collapsed to the cold, hard, mosaic-tiled floor, barely missing the guard's unsheathed, shining steel blade, which was aimed directly for Charmian's heart.

CHAPTER 29

A wash of Technicolor images flooded over Louise and swept her away. She saw the royal library on fire and the burning of thousands of scrolls into a pile of ash. She saw Cleopatra standing next to a silver-haired general in a red cloak raising a baby in the air for all of Egypt to see. She saw the queen wearing a headdress with three intertwined snakes sitting regally on a throne with a son on either side of her. She saw armies fighting, warships sinking, the crumbling destruction of the great towering lighthouse as it collapsed into the choppy water, and she watched as a snake curled up around Cleopatra's leg slithering up to her heart. Then a giant tidal wave rolled over the wide ancient streets and washed the great port city of Alexandria out into the bottom of the Mediterranean Sea.

*   *   *

Louise gasped for breath as though she were drowning. Her eyes flew open and for a flash she saw the angry, pursed red lips of Irene Sharaff yelling for her assistant. *"Joan!* Where did you go? Can we please get some work done around here? This is already the most expensive movie ever made without your antics! I need that belt immediately!"

I'm sorry, but I'm not Joan! Louise wanted to scream, but she couldn't speak. The sound of her voice got choked in her throat as she panicked, jumping up and desperately searching the wardrobe tent for the purple dress from the Fashionista Sale. She spotted it; a crumpled ball of silk dropped on the floor behind the rolling rack where she had changed earlier, and Louise quickly threw it back on over her clothes. As she fell deeper into the abyss, she found herself looking directly up into the unmistakable violet eyes of Dame Elizabeth Taylor sparkling at her, laughing, and then before she could so much as ask for an autograph she was sucked back down once again into the vortex of blackness.

"We live not according to reason,
but according to fashion."

SENECA,
Roman philosopher
and statesman
(4 BC–AD 65)

CHAPTER 30

Louise opened her eyes just as Brooke burst into the store. "Lou, I made it! Why haven't you been responding to my texts? I bet you didn't even miss me! Wait, where are you?"

"Over here," Louise's voice croaked, desperate for a glass of water. It turned out her best friend had made it after all.

"Ooh, I *love* that dress!" Brooke said, looking down at her.

Louise cracked a smile and rubbed her throbbing temples, so happy and relieved to be looking at her friend's familiar face and not Cleopatra's. "I was going to wear it to your dinner. What do you think?"

"It's awesome, and I think Peter will definitely approve," Brooke replied with a giggle. Louise felt her cheeks burning up.

"What did you do to your eyes?" Louise asked. Brooke's pale blue eyes were lined in dark black liner that was eerily reminiscent of the era Louise had just returned from.

"Just experimenting with makeup. I saw it in a magazine. Do you think it's too dramatic?" she asked.

"It's nice. I can give you a few tips," Louise said knowingly.

"You can?" Brooke asked, surprised since Louise wasn't even allowed to wear makeup yet. Brooke turned toward Marla and Glenda, who were hovering nearby. "Do you have another of those in pink? Maybe I'll get one, too. And why are you on the floor, Lou?" she asked, shifting her attention back to Louise, who was in fact still sitting in a pile of lavender silk. Helping Louise up from the dressing room floor and onto her shaky legs, Brooke gave her friend a questioning look. "You really shouldn't do that. It'll get wrinkled."

"It's one of a kind, dahling. That's the beauty of vintage: You can't just order it off a rack," Marla interrupted, pouring Louise a glass of water from a blue ceramic pitcher. Just looking at that jug made Louise's muscles ache—she was definitely glad to be back home, where the most that was required of her was to refill the Brita.

"The early bird gets the worm, as they say. Or the Yves Saint Laurent, as I say. Now, let's find something fabulous for you to wear! These dungarees are so déclassé!" Marla and Glenda guided Brooke in her heather gray tank top and skinny jeans to the other side of the store as Louise, still in a daze, drank the cool water in two refreshing gulps. She changed out of the long pleated gown and back into her hot pink Chuck Taylors

and blue paisley Laura Ashley sundress. It felt as if she were recovering from the worst jet lag ever. In a way, she supposed she was.

Louise glanced at her familiar reflection in the changing-room mirror. Unfortunately, the zit on her chin had come back to the twenty-first century with her. *Ugh*, apparently time travel was not good for the complexion. She also realized she was still wearing the pearl necklace from the wardrobe tent clasped around her neck. She fingered the large smooth orb and thought for a second about keeping it. It could probably pay for her college tuition. Actually, it could probably pay for the entire college. But, just as quickly, she decided against it. It felt wrong to have that in her private collection, besides the fact that it wasn't really hers, and she did *not* want to end up in ancient times again.

"Excuse me, I found this... in a trunk," she said as she took off the illicit ancient artifact and handed Glenda the necklace. Marla's eyes gleamed with approval, and Louise knew that finally she had made the right decision.

"Thank you, sweet pea. We've been looking all over for that." Glenda chuckled. "For quite a long time, in fact. Now, I think it's best if you two head home. You don't want your dear mother to be any more worried about you than she already is. Shall we wrap that gown up for you? It seemed to fit you rather well."

With a noticeable sigh of relief, Brooke took off the floppy Kentucky Derby–style hat piled high with pink feathers and ribbon that she had been reluctantly dressed in.

"Yes, please." Louise handed over the dress and tried not to laugh as the salesladies frantically ran around the shop looking for tissue paper and shopping bags in the oddest places. Somehow a customer making an actual purchase always seemed to catch them off guard.

"Oh, dear, how about we put it in this instead?" a frazzled Marla asked as she rolled the gown into a giant messy ball and shoved it into a large buttery vintage Birkin bag that was hanging on a nearby coat tree.

"Works for me!" Louise replied quickly as Brooke looked on wide-eyed. Even though Brooke wasn't into used clothes, she wasn't one to turn down a free Hermès bag, either. Even if it was from the seventies.

Bring bring briiiing! Louise was startled to hear the sound of an old-fashioned telephone ringing from the depths of the shop. It seemed odd that such a temporary store would have a landline.

"Oh, my, who on earth could that be?" Glenda looked at Marla with an alarmed expression.

"Are you expecting anyone, dahling?" Marla asked Louise, puzzled.

"And where did we put the phone?" Glenda scrambled in

the direction of the incessant ringing, finally uncovering a black rotary phone hidden under a pile of dark brown mink stoles.

"Fashionista Vintage Sale, how may I direct your call?" Glenda asked, pausing, her cat green eyes growing wide with alarm. "She's where?" Glenda trilled.

Marla rushed over to her and leaned her mousy head in close to the receiver so she could hear as well. The two anxious women shooed their only customers out of the store with a distracted wave without so much as saying good-bye.

CHAPTER 31

After that unsettling exit, the girls silently walked home from the shop. Louise adjusted her newly acquired Birkin bag on her shoulder, feeling immensely relieved to be back in her old hometown with her best friend, who, not surprisingly, had left the sale empty-handed. Each adventure seemed to be getting progressively more dangerous, and this one was a particularly close call.

"Sorry for not answering your texts. I'm really glad you came. I know that vintage shopping is not exactly your favorite weekend activity," Louise apologized, kicking a rock with the toe of her pink sneaker.

"I wouldn't miss it for all the lacrosse games in the world," Brooke joked. "Sorry for being so late."

"So, how's Kip?" Louise asked, realizing this was the first time she had actually initiated a conversation with Brooke about her new boyfriend. Maybe she hadn't been that good of a friend herself. "Did they win?"

"Yes, it was such a good game!" Brooke started excitedly. "And he looks so cute in his lacrosse uniform. There's this guy Nathan Waters on his team who lives in Eastport that you might like. Maybe we can all hang out together sometime."

"That's okay." Louise smiled. She was happy for her friend but didn't really have any desire for a boyfriend herself right now. The guys she had met recently—Benjamin Guggenheim, Louis XVI, Ptolemy—they just seemed to make life way too complicated.

"Right, you're too busy deciding between Todd Berkowitz and my cousin Peter," Brooke teased. Louise smiled, but stayed silent. The real reason was way too complicated to explain right now.

"And now that you have this all-consuming vintage obsession, at least I'll have someone to hang out with," Brooke said teasingly, although Louise could detect a hint of sadness in the way she said it. Maybe it wasn't all a joke; maybe her best friend was just as scared of losing her. She had never thought about it that way before.

"Brooke, I am not ditching you for some old clothes," Louise said, laughing and throwing her arms around her oldest ally. "You're always my best friend. I mean, we've known each other forever. Our lives are, like, permanently linked together." The girls hooked arms and continued walking toward home, both closer and further apart than they had ever been before.

*   *   *

When Louise finally walked in the front door of the Lamberts' rambling Tudor-style home, she was surprised to find the house eerily empty. "Hello, anybody home? Mom? Dad?" she yelled out into the large, drafty foyer. Silence. This wasn't the concerned, overbearing welcome she was expecting—apparently her parents weren't so worried about her after all. She checked the time on her cell and realized that even though it felt as if she'd been gone for eons, it had really been only a few hours since she had taken off for the Fashionista Sale that morning. She ran upstairs, excited to dive into her research. She needed to know exactly what she had just been through.

When Louise reached into her soft leather Birkin bag to hang up her dress, a small coin fell out from between the folds of the fabric. She picked up what felt like a misshapen penny from her bedroom floor and discovered that it was actually a small bronze coin with the profile of a woman on it. On closer examination, she saw that it was in fact Cleopatra's now-familiar profile—her long hook nose, thick neck, and pronounced chin, hair in a bun tied back with a band of ribbon, exactly like the woman Louise just met! She smiled, noticing that it was Cleopatra's profile, not Ptolemy's nor Arsinoe's stamped on the currency. She had gotten her wish

215

after all! It would be her good-luck charm, Louise decided. Just rubbing it between her two fingers gave her a poised and powerful feeling, as though some of Cleopatra's confidence could transfer to her through the metal. Marla and Glenda must have slipped it into the bag when she wasn't looking.

Louise reverently placed the Egyptian currency in her vanity drawer along with the diamond-tipped hairpin from Versailles and the newspaper photograph from the *Titanic*. Like Irene Sharaff, she was starting her own little collection of keepsakes, a way for her to always remember her past adventures.

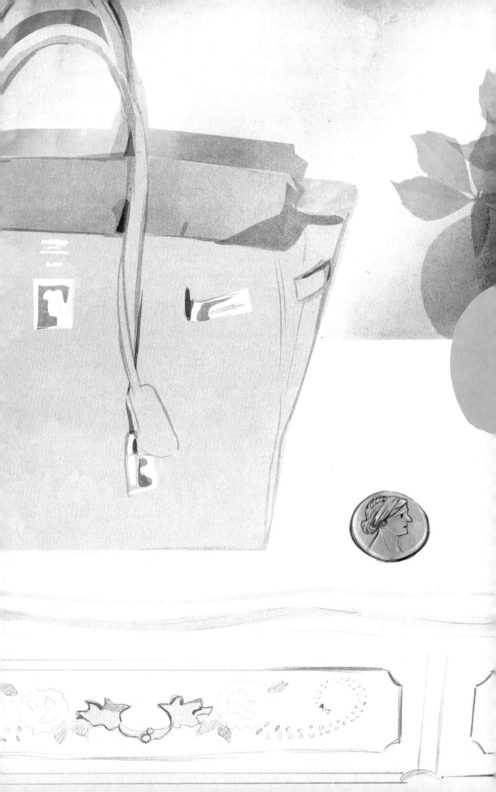

CHAPTER 32

Louise opened her laptop and eagerly dove into her research on Cleopatra. She wished she could get as excited about her homework assignments at school, but sometimes it was hard to see how the Pythagorean theorem related to her real life. These historical events felt as if they *were* her real life. After a few basic Internet searches, she was taken aback to find that this particular investigation wasn't quite as easy as she had anticipated. When she had looked up the *Titanic* and the French Revolution, there had been a ton of material online for her to sort through: scanned original documents, articles, photographs, and newspaper interviews with firsthand accounts. But Louise quickly discovered that very little from Cleopatra's time had survived, and absolutely nothing written by the Egyptian queen's own hand. Louise thought back to the scroll of poisons that Cleopatra was compiling and got chills thinking that no one but her would ever know about that. In fact, even the streets of ancient Alexandria that Louise had just walked down no longer existed. The whole city was apparently wiped out because of constant military battles and natural disasters.

ALEXANDRIA WAS BOTH THE CULTURAL AND INTELLECTUAL CAPITAL OF THE ANCIENT WORLD, WHERE PHILOSOPHERS, ASTRONOMERS, AND DOCTORS WOULD COME TOGETHER AT THE ROYAL LIBRARY TO SHARE IDEAS, AND MANY OF THE GREAT PHILOSOPHIES AND THEOREMS WERE HATCHED THERE. THE GRAND LIBRARY INADVERTENTLY BURNED TO THE GROUND WHEN JULIUS CAESAR SET A FLEET OF SHIPS IN THE HARBOR ON FIRE AND THE UNCONTROLLABLE FLAMES SPREAD THROUGHOUT THE CITY. WITH IT, THOUSANDS OF IRREPLACEABLE SCROLLS AND TEXTS WERE DESTROYED.

AFTER CLEOPATRA'S DEFEAT BY THE ROMAN LEADER OCTAVIAN IN 30 BC, HER CONQUEROR ORDERED EVERYTHING OF HERS TO BE DESTROYED, INCLUDING ALL HER DETAILED JOURNALS. AS A RESULT, EVERYTHING WRITTEN ABOUT THE MOST FAMOUS QUEEN OF THE ANCIENT WORLD WAS PUT DOWN ON PAPER MORE THAN ONE HUNDRED YEARS AFTER HER DEATH, MOST NOTABLY BY THE GREEK HISTORIAN PLUTARCH:

"FOR HER BEAUTY, AS WE ARE TOLD, WAS IN ITSELF NOT ALTOGETHER INCOMPARABLE, NOR SUCH AS TO STRIKE THOSE WHO SAW HER; BUT TO CONVERSE WITH HER HAD AN IRRESISTIBLE CHARM, AND HER PRESENCE, COMBINED WITH THE PERSUASIVENESS OF HER DISCOURSE AND THE CHARACTER

WHICH WAS SOMEHOW DIFFUSED ABOUT HER BEHAVIOUR TOWARDS OTHERS, HAD SOMETHING STIMULATING ABOUT IT. THERE WAS SWEETNESS ALSO IN THE TONES OF HER VOICE; AND HER TONGUE, LIKE AN INSTRUMENT OF MANY STRINGS, SHE COULD READILY TURN TO WHATEVER LANGUAGE SHE PLEASED..."—PLUTARCH, *LIFE OF ANTONY*

UNFORTUNATELY FOR CLEOPATRA, HER HISTORY WAS WRITTEN BY MEN WITH THEIR OWN AGENDAS, MANY WHO WERE HER ENEMIES. FOR THIS REASON, SHE HAS BEEN PORTRAYED AS A SEDUCTRESS, EVIL, AND OVERLY DRAMATIC.

Louise now knew firsthand that these unflattering descriptions had nothing to do with the intelligent leader's actual character.

After her first never-ending day in the ancient classroom, Louise was hardly surprised to read that Cleopatra was extremely educated and spoke at least nine languages fluently. *Amazing*, Louise thought. She often felt as if she could barely master English.

AS WAS THE CUSTOM, CLEOPATRA PRESENTED HERSELF AS THE HUMAN EMBODIMENT OF THE FERTILITY GODDESS ISIS AND WAS WORSHIPPED BY THE PEOPLE. THIS CLOSE ASSOCIATION WITH THE DEITY GAVE HER EVEN MORE POLITICAL CLOUT, AND WHENEVER THERE WAS AN OFFICIAL CEREMONY SHE WOULD DRESS AS THE GODDESS IN PUBLIC. SHE WAS ALSO THE FIRST MEMBER OF HER GREEK FAMILY TO SPEAK

EGYPTIAN SO THAT SHE COULD ACTUALLY COMMUNICATE
WITH THE PEOPLE OF THE LAND SHE WAS RULING.

It was reassuring for Louise that the most powerful woman of the ancient world, and maybe ever, didn't get to that position through her looks as history and Hollywood made it seem. She was a skilled politician, a great public speaker, and an extremely motivated student who tried to learn as much as she could get her hands on. And not being traditionally beautiful with a particularly large nose, crooked teeth, and frizzy hair didn't get in her way. Being smart was pretty cool after all.

Louise kept reading.

BECAUSE OF THE SCORCHING DESERT HEAT AND RAMPANT LICE PROBLEM, WIGS WERE VERY POPULAR, AND HAIR REMOVAL WAS EXTREMELY IMPORTANT TO THE EGYPTIANS.

She instinctively reached up to her own hair, half surprised not to knock off Charmian's wig. Nope, for better or worse, her curly tangles were back. As she read on, she found that most people of the time shaved their heads and protected themselves from the sun with a wide array of decorative wigs and thick kohl eye makeup, as she'd guessed.

ALTHOUGH MANY MEMBERS OF THE ROYAL FAMILY WORE CROWNS, THE TRIPLE URANUS, A CROWN WITH THREE SNAKES INTERTWINED, WAS UNIQUE TO CLEOPATRA, AND FROM THAT PIECE OF HEADWEAR ARCHAEOLOGISTS COULD DETERMINE

WHAT SCULPTURES ARE MOST LIKELY REPRESENTATIONS OF THE POWERFUL QUEEN.

The Triple Uranus must have been the headpiece that Cleopatra wore to the dinner with the Roman general!

AFTER HER FATHER'S DEATH, CLEOPATRA WAS MARRIED TO HER TEN-YEAR-OLD YOUNGER BROTHER, PTOLEMY, WHO WAS TO BE HER CO-RULER. ALTHOUGH THIS MAY SEEM STRANGE TO A MODERN AUDIENCE, CLEOPATRA'S PARENTS WERE ALSO SIBLINGS, AND THIS MARRIAGE WITH CLOSE RELATIONS HAPPENED QUITE FREQUENTLY, SO THAT THE FAMILY COULD KEEP ITS POWER CONTAINED. HOWEVER, THIS SYSTEM CAUSED ITS OWN SETS OF PROBLEMS, AS FAMILY MEMBERS WERE CONSTANTLY MURDERING AND PLOTTING TO GET RID OF THEIR OWN BLOOD RELATIVES. IT WAS NOT UNCOMMON FOR SIBLINGS TO KILL EACH OTHER, AND CLEOPATRA WAS THE ONLY PERSON IN HER KNOTTY FAMILY TREE WHO WAS NOT KILLED BY A CLOSE FAMILIAL RELATION. SHE DIED BY HER OWN CHOICE IN WHAT HAS BECOME A FAMOUS LEGEND IMMORTALIZED BY EVERYONE FROM SHAKESPEARE TO HOLLYWOOD DIRECTORS. CLEOPATRA COMMITTED SUICIDE BY ASP BITE AFTER DISCOVERING THE DEATH OF HER TRUE LOVE, MARC ANTONY, AND THE FALL OF ALEXANDRIA TO THE ROMANS. THE YOUNG QUEEN WAS NEARLY THIRTY-NINE YEARS OLD WHEN SHE DIED IN 30 BC.

Louise realized that what she saw with the prisoner must have been Cleopatra researching her plans for her own death one day! So that was what the queen had meant when she'd said she wanted to control her own fate.

Louise next decided to google "Cleopatra Movie" to see if she could find out more behind-the-scenes gossip.

CLEOPATRA WAS PRODUCED FOR WHAT TODAY WOULD BE $323 MILLION AND STILL REMAINS THE MOST EXPENSIVE MOVIE EVER MADE IN THE HISTORY OF CINEMA. THE STRESS OF THE PUBLIC SCRUTINY AND NUMEROUS HOLDUPS IN PRODUCTION NEARLY KILLED DIRECTOR JOSEPH MANKIEWICZ. HE HAD A RARE SKIN CONDITION THAT CAUSED HIS FINGERS TO SPLIT OPEN DURING TIMES OF STRESS, AND THEREFORE WAS REQUIRED BY HIS PHYSICIAN TO WEAR WHITE GLOVES WHILE SHOOTING. AT THE PREMIERE OF THE MOVIE, WHEN ASKED BY A REPORTER HOW HE FELT ABOUT THE FIRST SCREENING OF THE FILM, MR. MANKIEWICZ RESPONDED GLUMLY, "I FEEL LIKE THE GUILLOTINE IS ABOUT TO DROP."

THE FILM IS ALSO NOTABLY KNOWN TO BE THE PLACE WHERE STARS ELIZABETH TAYLOR AND RICHARD BURTON MET FOR THE FIRST TIME AND BEGAN ONE OF THE MOST FAMOUS AND TUMULTUOUS AFFAIRS IN HOLLYWOOD HISTORY, RESULTING IN THEIR MARRYING EACH OTHER TWICE AND DRAMATICALLY BREAKING UP COUNTLESS TIMES.

Louise then clicked on a link for "Irene Sharaff," excited to learn more about her former boss. She was still a little annoyed at herself that she had only experienced a tiny bit of the best summer internship ever. She had totally blown it by taking that necklace. Oh, well. She learned her lesson.

Irene Sharaff was one of the most talented costume designers ever to work behind the scenes of Hollywood and Broadway. She was a five-time Academy Award winner and worked with all of the most famous actors, actresses, and ballerinas of her time, including Elizabeth Taylor, Rita Hayworth, Barbra Streisand, and Judy Garland. The costume budget for Ms. Taylor on the film *Cleopatra* was the largest for any actress at that time, and the dozens of dresses Miss Sharaff designed for her included one made with real gold.

Louise was excited to read that Irene started out as a fashion illustrator for *Vogue* magazine before switching careers and moving to Paris to study and become a costume designer. Maybe all of Louise's dress-designing doodles were a step in the right direction. Who knew where they would take her!

In the midst of her intensive research, Louise was startled by the ping of a new e-mail landing in her inbox. She clicked over to her Gmail and was excited to see that it was a message from Stella!

Hey, Louise,
Sorry for not responding sooner, but I've been sort of held up by a little Civil War. LONG story, but watch out for those cute vintage

military jackets—you never know where they'll lead you. Would love to catch up! Seems like we're cut from the same cloth. See you at the next sale, dahling! xoxo, Stella

Louise grinned; it was the right Stella after all! She couldn't wait to tell her fellow Fashionista about hanging out with Cleopatra and Elizabeth Taylor.

Hey, Stella,
YES, can't wait to see you and go vintage shopping! I've recently developed a new appreciation for pearls. I never realized their history was so...ancient. And did you know that Elizabeth Taylor really did have purple eyes? Will tell you the rest at the sale!
BTW, be careful of those fabulous Grecian dresses—they may not actually be Greek!
Your fellow Fashionista, Louise Lambert

Louise responded immediately, and then instantly regretted not waiting a day so that she wouldn't seem too desperate for friends. Ugh, oh, well. Playing it cool had never been her strength.

"Honey, we're home!" her parents called up to her as the heavy front door locked behind them. "Can you come downstairs for a moment? We have something to discuss with you in the living room!"

"Sure, be right there!" Louise yelled through her closed bedroom door. Discussions in the formal living room were never a good sign, but these time-traveling adventures always made her a little homesick and she was excited to hear her parents' familiar voices. Even if she was going to be in trouble for going to the Fashionista Sale. Or maybe they had somehow found out about the pearl necklace! Louise shut her laptop and ran downstairs, eager to see her now seemingly normal family. At least they weren't out to murder one another for political gain. She was starting to appreciate the small things...

"I have some good news, and I have some bad news," her father announced, leaning back into the uncomfortable white sofa that they never used except for occasional entertaining and family meetings. Louise held her breath trying to think of all the bad things that could possibly have happened.

"The good news is, I have an offer with Swanson & Gordon Attorneys here in Fairview. The bad news is, the wild mushroom risotto I was about to tackle needs to be put on the back burner, so to speak. Although I won't have such a long commute, and I should be able to occasionally cook dinner, I think I'll have to hang up the apron for now," he added, removing his wire-rimmed glasses and polishing them on his classic blue Oxford shirt.

"Isn't that wonderful, dahling?" Mrs. Lambert asked

Louise, a little too enthusiastically. Her mother looked totally relieved, and for once the strand of ivory pearls looped around her neck was not twisted into a luxurious noose between her fidgety fingers. Louise didn't think she'd ever be able to look at pearls the same way again.

"It has only been a few days. You'd think I've been out of work for a year," her father replied jokingly as he put his arm around his wife, who was wearing a peach cashmere cardigan and cream-colored slacks, sitting with perfect posture at the edge of the pristinely upholstered couch.

"Congrats! That's great, Dad!" Louise exclaimed, happy to see her parents in such a good mood and totally relieved that she wasn't in any trouble herself. Although she was definitely not thrilled to be back to a life of boiled potatoes soaked in malt vinegar. After all, if a cup of vinegar could dissolve a pearl, imagine what it was doing to her stomach. She smiled, feeling lucky and happy to be back home.

CHAPTER 33

That night there was a sharp knock on Louise's bedroom door.

"Dahling, can I come in?" her mother whispered from the hall.

Louise definitely wasn't sleeping. Now that she was safe and back home in her familiar bedroom, the whole time-traveling experience was starting to feel more and more like a distant dream. But after everything she had just experienced in Hollywood and Alexandria, witnessing two deaths and having a sharp steel sword aimed directly for her own heart not that long ago, it was going to take her a while to feel totally relaxed. "Yeah, Mom, I'm awake."

Mrs. Lambert, in her periwinkle blue pajama set with white piping, perched herself at the foot of Louise's canopy bed and began playing with a loose thread on her worn patch-work quilt. "I think we need to have a chat. I suppose I should have had this talk with you before, but as you can imagine it's not the easiest conversation to begin."

"Great," Louise enthused, propping herself up on her elbows, ready to finally get some answers to the questions that had been boggling her mind for the past week.

"Where to begin?" her mother mused, looking off into the distance.

"Are you a Traveling Fashionista?" Louise asked, cutting right to the chase. She didn't want to lose her mother to one of these internal reveries again. "Is that why you have that necklace? And that old photograph? Was that really you in that picture?"

Louise's mom chuckled slightly at her daughter's enthusiasm. "I suppose at one point I was. My aunt Alice took me to my first Fashionista Sale in London. Glenda and Marla used to do all her costumes. She was an actress, as I know you've discovered."

"So you *do* know Marla and Glenda!" Louise exclaimed, trying to fit all the puzzle pieces together in her head.

"Yes, but I couldn't let you know that, dahling. How else do you think they were able to find our address when they delivered you home after your first sale? GPS?" Mrs. Lambert laughed again and Louise joined in. The thought of Marla and Glenda using a modern tracking device was preposterous. "I've had quite a few adventures in my day. But that's all in the past now. Those are stories for another time."

"But why did you stop?" Louise asked, not able to comprehend how you could just give up such an amazing double life. She wanted to go and experience as many other lives and histories as she could, for as long as she could, even if it was dangerous sometimes.

"Well, when you have a child, you can't exactly take off for another century. Somehow time-traveling between PTA meetings seemed a little odd. What if something happened to me in the past? Marla and Glenda are very cautious, but there's always a small chance, and I couldn't risk it."

Louise protectively wrapped her arms around herself at the thought of losing her mother to the bubonic plague or Hindenburg disaster or in some other distant tragedy. It was too sad to think about. "Thank you," she finally mumbled.

"So, I decided to start living in the present, and for once really enjoy and experience what will one day be history for somebody else. You may not appreciate it yet, but today can be just as exciting as yesterday. Oh, Louise, you should have seen London in the eighties. It was marvelous!" her mom exclaimed, her eyes sparkling at the memory. "Well, perhaps one day you will...."

"I hope so," Louise said, already lost in the fantasy of getting her hands on a Vivienne Westwood minikilt.

"Clothes have special power. They are loaded with memory. It can be very dangerous. I didn't want to encourage you.

And yet you can't stop someone from realizing her destiny. I suppose our old movie nights are the one way that I can get a little taste of the past without leaving our couch, and get the chance to share that with you. That's why they're so precious to me. You're more like me than you realize," she said, giving Louise's foot a little squeeze through the blankets.

On the outside, Louise didn't look like her mom, always put-together with her ash blonde perfectly coiffed hair and matching sweater sets compared with Louise's auburn frizzy mess and crazy thrift-store outfits. But maybe on the inside they were alike after all.

"So it runs in our family?" Louise asked sleepily, as much as she was fighting to keep her eyelids open, her mother's soothing English accent slowly pulling her into a dream world.

"I suppose it does, I suppose it does."

CHAPTER 34

At the last minute on Monday morning, Louise decided to wear the poodle charm necklace to school under her dress, a secret reminder of who she really was in the midst of an ordinary day of junior high. Although she was obviously still a seventh-grade student at Fairview, Louise was also a Traveling Fashionista, and in the monotonous and often embarrassing details of her daily life, it was too easy to forget that. She also attempted to add a touch of dark gray eyeliner to her lids as Cleopatra did, but glancing in the mirror she had to admit it wasn't quite Elizabeth Taylor–worthy. It still looked kind of nice, though. She just had to make sure not to run into her parents on the way out the door, as they would most likely have a different opinion on the matter.

She snapped a Polaroid, happily knowing that this morning there would actually be a slight change in her appearance even if it was just from a little makeup. Louise opened her sock drawer and took out the Polaroid she had shot the other morning. Just as she'd thought, in her rush, she had aimed the camera too low. Half of her head was cut off, leaving only her closed, tight-lipped smile and the top of her green dress. Her trademark hair was pulled back out of the shot, and for a second it was almost as if she were looking at someone else. For the first time, she realized that she and her mother had the same mouth, and if Louise looked quickly, she could almost be mistaken for a younger version of her mother in this photo. Weird. She always thought she could have been adopted, never seeing the resemblance between them. But she was definitely her mother's daughter—the braces had gotten in the way of her being able to see that. She shoved the photo back into the drawer, tucked the charm necklace discreetly under her Peter Pan collar, and ran out to catch the bus.

On the ride to school that morning, when Billy popped up behind their bus seat for his daily sarcastic commentary, Louise was ready for him. She rubbed the ancient coin in her pocket for an extra boost of courage, feeling the ridges of Cleopatra's profile with her thumb, and then turned around and looked her greasy-haired tormentor directly in the eye. "No one has ever asked for your fashion advice. *Ever.* So keep it to yourself. We're not interested. Leave us alone."

She saw Brooke's eyes widen with surprise at Louise's new-found confidence, and then her friend broke into a huge grin. "Ditto to what she said," Brooke added.

"Sorry, Louise, you know I was just kidding. Jeez." He slunk off to the back of the bus, and for the first time Louise realized that if he wasn't tormenting her, Billy Robertson actually didn't have anyone else to talk to. Maybe teasing her was the only way that he didn't have to sit totally alone.

When she got to school, Louise was surprised to see that Todd was waiting for her at her locker.

"Are you wearing makeup?" he asked, brushing his dark wavy hair out of his eyes to get a better look.

"A little," Louise replied. For some illogical reason, she was embarrassed that he'd noticed.

"No, I mean, it's good. But you don't really need it," he said, studying her face as if she were a totally different person.

"Thanks?" Louise replied at his backhanded compliment. "You're kind of blocking my locker, though." He casually moved and leaned against Brooke's locker.

"Sorry, so anyway, if you're not busy, maybe we can do something or something."

Louise smiled at his muddled invitation to do . . . she wasn't sure what. Maybe he was just odd and awkward, as she was sometimes. And then it hit her—maybe there really was nothing to *get*. "Sure, Todd, that sounds cool," she replied, not overthinking it.

"What's that necklace?" he asked. Louise looked down and saw that the charm necklace had popped out from beneath her collar.

"Just something my mom gave me," Louise said, tucking it back in. It seemed so private to her; she forgot that other people could see it, too.

"It's different. I like it. Anyways, I'll see you later, then," Todd said, getting on his skateboard and taking off through the crowded hall. He nearly ran into Miss Jones, Louise's history class substitute, who looked just as frazzled as she did on her first day. Louise laughed, happy that some things never changed.

CHAPTER 35

"I heard at the PTA meeting that your history teacher Miss Morris just packed up and left for vacation before the year was over. I never considered her much of a traveler. Isn't that rather peculiar? And right before the end of the school year. How do you like the sub?" Mrs. Lambert asked on the drive over to the Pattersons' dinner party that evening.

"Miss Jones is great—she started showing us the movie *Cleopatra* in class."

"Oh, I love that film. That's always been one of my favorites. I can't believe I never watched that with you. The costumes were fabulous from what I remember," she said, touching up her makeup in the visor mirror. "Actually, your dress probably could have been in that movie. That seemed to be the style of the times."

"Who knows? Maybe it was," Louise replied with a wink. "Did you know Irene Sharaff won an Academy Award for her work on that movie? She was one of the best costume designers of all time."

"How did you know that?" her mom asked, looking over her shoulder to the backseat.

"It's kind of a long story," Louise said, shaking her head. "I feel like there's a lot we need to catch up on."

"I imagine there is," her mother replied, nervously looking over at Mr. Lambert, who was totally oblivious and whistling along off-key to some oldie that was playing on the radio.

Her parents' Volvo pulled up the long car-filled driveway to the Pattersons' familiar Colonial-style house, and Louise got a few butterflies thinking about seeing Peter again outside of school. As she had suspected, her parents hadn't let her wear any eyeliner, but she still felt as though she looked pretty good. Her curly hair was tied up in a low bun with a white ribbon holding back the wisps the same way Cleopatra had worn it. She was wearing a pair of gladiator sandals, but these were from Steve Madden, not ancient Egypt, and were a million times more comfortable. Looking down at her lavender pleated dress, she got a jolt of confidence. She realized she would probably never be the most beautiful girl in the room, particularly compared with her naturally gorgeous best friend, but she knew she had something special inside her, a unique set of experiences that would help guide her and give her confidence in her day-to-day life.

"That's a great dress," Peter commented when the Lamberts walked into the Pattersons' crowded living room. Louise's lavender hem swept the polished hardwood floor. Her mom and dad rushed off in the other direction to say hello to Brooke's parents. "Like something out of an old movie or something. In a good way," he added, almost sounding a bit nervous.

"Thanks, it's vintage," Louise responded confidently, but with a few little butterflies still fluttering around her stomach thanks to Peter's dimpled smile. She had almost forgotten how cute he was.

"Told you he'd like it," Brooke teased, grabbing a pig in a blanket from a white-smocked caterer who was circling the room with a tray of appetizers. Louise instinctively knocked the bite-size hot dog out of her friend's pink manicured fingers thinking for a second that it could be poisoned, before realizing that she was back in the twenty-first century and that no one was trying to kill them with hors d'oeuvres.

"Sorry," Louise apologized, once again mortified. "Arm spasm."

Brooke observed Louise with a confused expression and then grabbed a miniquiche from the next waiter who passed by. She looked amazing as usual with her long blonde layers perfectly framing her face and wearing a short white lace dress with a black satin bow tied around her waist. There was no question that Brooke was her mother's daughter, though. And Mrs. Patterson, with the youthful looks of someone who was constantly declared Brooke's "sister," must have invited half of Fairview to the dinner. Even the mayor was holding court by the buffet table.

"Everything Louise owns is vintage," Brooke said, rolling her eyes after swallowing the tiny bite of quiche.

"Sweet," Peter said. "I think it's great that you don't dress like a clone of everyone else here," he said, jokingly punching his cousin in the arm. "Maybe you can help me find some vintage stuff. My parents threw out half of my clothes when we moved." Louise noticed that he was wearing the same old-fashioned-looking charcoal gray three-piece suit that he wore to Brooke's thirteenth birthday party a few weeks ago. For once, Louise felt happy about standing out.

"Sure," she replied. "That would be fun." She would not overanalyze whether this was a date, she thought, clearly already overanalyzing.

"You should take him to—" Brooke began.

"I can take you to the Salvation Army downtown," Louise interrupted. "And I'm an expert eBay and Etsy shopper."

Brooke raised her eyebrow and gave her another quizzical look, but she didn't push the issue. Louise liked Peter and felt as though she could trust him, but she wasn't ready to share

her ultimate vintage source with anyone besides her best friend. Maybe one day she would take him to meet Marla and Glenda, but not yet.

Louise felt a slight tug on the skirt of her dress, and she turned around to find Brooke's eight-year-old brother scowling up at her from under his mop of flaxen blond curls, poking her with a light-up blue plastic sword. "This is so boring. Will you play with me, Lou?"

"Maybe later," Louise acquiesced, feeling a stomach-churning wave of déjà vu. Apparently younger brothers were annoying whatever century you were in.

"Please?" he whined.

"Leave us alone, Julian," Brooke said, exasperated, swatting him away like a housefly. "Can't you see that we're in the middle of an important adult conversation?"

"It's not fair. You never want to play with me!" The towheaded boy stormed off in a huff, swinging his toy weapon, which made an automated clanging sound with each slice through the air.

And suddenly, as Louise grabbed a coconut shrimp skewer from another passing platter and watched Brooke's little brother weave through the legs of other partygoers, she had a startling realization. She had been so happy to be back to her normal life, and so excited to meet up with Stella again at the next Traveling Fashionista Vintage Sale, that she didn't notice she hadn't yet received an invitation.

ACKNOWLEDGMENTS

This book would not have been possible without the help of some fabulous fashionistas at Poppy, particularly my new partner in crime, Pam Gruber; Alison Impey; Lisa Moraleda; Mara Lander; Christine Ma; and Tracy Koontz. I think I may have the most supportive, patient, and hilarious agent in NYC, Elisabeth Weed. And I am forever grateful to Cindy Eagan for discovering and bringing Louise's story to life. Thanks to Howie Sanders and Dana Borowitz at UTA for making me feel glamorous by association.

Thank you to Carter Lupton at the Milwaukee Public Museum for being so generous with his time and archaeological expertise. You do officially have the coolest job ever! A very belated thanks to some early supporters of T-TF: Carolyn MacCullough for being such a great teacher, Sebastian Silva for sharing his *Titanic* knowledge and book collection, and Heather Dyer for reminding me what middle school is really like. Thanks to David Swanson, whose additional editing and creativity made this book even better than I had hoped for. Thank you to my extremely understanding cohorts at Schnabel Studio: Julian Schnabel, Tamiko Benjamin, Cat Yezbak, Gretchen Kraus, and Porfirio Munoz, who give me the time and flexibility to lead this amazing double life. Deepest gratitude to my grandmother Louise who has a drawer full of magical ideas just waiting to be developed, and the energy and enthusiasm to get me to do it. I can't wait to see where this next chapter takes us!

A NOTE FROM THE AUTHOR

I've always been captivated by the story of Cleopatra. My fascination began with reading Shakespeare's *Antony and Cleopatra* in my high school English class and continued through watching Elizabeth Taylor portray Egypt's most famous queen on the silver screen. During the research process for this book, I was surprised to discover how little is actually known about Cleopatra's reign in ancient Egypt. As it turns out, almost all of Cleopatra's writings and belongings were destroyed after the queen's death. Much of her story is left to speculation as archaeologists and historians try to reconstruct her incredible life from what artifacts and documents do remain. But rather than being problematic, this lack of information makes her life great fodder for a fiction writer like me! It leaves me plenty of room to take the pieces we do know for sure—like her marriage to Ptolemy, her younger brother and co-ruler, and his subsequent plot on her life—and imagine the rest of the details.

One of the more famous legends about Cleopatra—and my favorite—is the pearl-earring story woven into Chapter 26. Although the historical incident probably didn't take place until a few years later, I couldn't resist including it in my book. The "famous Roman general" visiting Egypt was actually Marc Antony, who met Cleopatra later in her life. I took the liberty of moving this event to this point in time to illustrate Cleopatra's character, cunning, and humor.

Cleopatra was once the richest and most influential person in the ancient world, and she reigned more than two thousand years ago. It's amazing how modern it seems to have a powerful woman ruling over a kingdom. I wanted to depict the famous Queen of the Nile as she *really* was: a smart and shrewd politician who spoke many languages and was probably not all that beautiful by today's standards. Hollywood has painted her as a gorgeous seductress, but historians now believe this wasn't quite the case. For me, imagining Cleopatra as a more ordinary-looking person, as seen in her portrait profile on her coin, is both more impressive and more relatable, making Cleopatra someone who could truly inspire a budding fashionista like Louise and, I hope, my readers.

Explore ancient Egypt and learn even more
about Cleopatra with these resources!

BOOKS:

Cleopatra: A Life, by Stacy Schiff

Antony and Cleopatra, by William Shakespeare

The Royal Diaries, Cleopatra VII: Daughter of the Nile, by Kristiana Gregory

Cleopatra: Last Queen of Egypt, by Joyce Tyldesley

Cleopatra, by Diane Stanley and Peter Vennema

Cleopatra and Rome, by Diana E. E. Kleiner

MOVIES:

Cleopatra, directed by Joseph L. Makiewicz (Twentieth Century Fox Film Corporation, 1963). (Featuring Elizabeth Taylor)

Cleopatra: The First Woman of Power, directed by Katherine Gilday, narrated by Anjelica Huston (CineNova Productions Inc., 1999).